LOVE AT
FIRST NIGHT

LOVE AT FIRST NIGHT

PRATIK HINDOCHA

PARTRIDGE
A Penguin Company

Partridge books may be ordered through booksellers or by contacting:

Partridge India
Phone: 000.800.10062.62

I would like to take this opportunity to thank my parents for all their love, and their constant and unconditional support.

I would also like thank my editor Sonal Patel for the trouble she took in editing this book and to my literature tutor, Mrs. Namita Khurana for her special support, and to my publishers and to each and everyone who encouraged me write this book.

My grandmother who passed away while I busy
writing this book . . .

SHE SHALL ALWAYS LIVE IN OUR HEARTS.

And to my parents

.

.

.

"DON'T CRY WHEN SOMEBODY LEAVES YOU, CRY WHEN YOU LEAVE SOMEBODY WHO HAS TRULY EVER LOVED YOU"

—PRATIK HINDOCHA

SPECIAL NOTE

The SYMBOLS above the quotations in the earlier page are the same quotationswritten in a symbolic language and the same method is used for the other quotations written ahead in the book

CHAPTER 1

"Granny!", shouted a small and fair little kid in black shorts and white t-shirt. He ran to his old granny who sat on the wooden bench over the short green grass of the garden in the early Sunday morning, in a plain white shirt, with a silver sweater over it and a black track pant. And the yellow rays of the sun fell right on her face.

The old woman was lost in her thoughts as she looked at the happy young couples who were in the garden for their early morning jog, or were performing light exercises and yoga together or along with their small kids in the fresh open-air. She looked at the big trees with green leaves, and the sun shining right above them.

Her heart was glum; it wasn't hurt by anyone but it was desolately due to the loss it had to suffer, some precious gem, which it lost: the gem of love and protection.

Her cute grandson, who brings a bit of a smile to her face every day and becomes an excuse to make her heart happy, sidetracked the old lady from her thoughts.

She looked at him as he reached her and gave him a forceful smile.

"Hey honey, why is my little boy so excited?' her grandson stops in-front of her (breathing heavily), 'Looks like you have brought something for your granny, haven't you?', the old lady asked, as she saw the locked palms of her grandson.

"Yes, grandma, I just found something really exciting on the backside of the garden," replied the boy with his cute smile.

"Oh, wouldn't you like to show it to your old granny then?" asked the old lady.

"Not before you close your eyes," replied her grandson.

"Okay my naughty boy, but don't make your granny wait for long," said the old lady and she closed her eyes and saw the darkness.Her grandson then opened his palms and asked her to open her eyes.

She slowly opened her eyes and the darkness of her eyes be replaced with the light of the sun. Tears rolled out through her eyes as she saw colorful shells in the palms of her grandson. The shells were very precious to her and held an important place in her memories, which was why her heart was again burdened with emotions.

'What happened grandma? Why do you cry? Did I do something wrong? Don't you like them?,' asked her curious grandson as he saw a tear rolling out of her eyes.

'No honey, they are so beautiful, I used to love them a lot,' replied the old lady 'where are your mummy and daddy sweetie?'

'They have gone for a walk on the beach behind the garden,' replied the boy.

'And don't you want to join them,' asked the old lady.

'No grandma I want to hear some nice stories from you,' replied the boy.

'Oh, is that so? Well then I will have to think of some nice little story for my cute little boy,' said the old lady 'so you wait awhile till I remember one'.

There were no more words between both of them for a while. The little guy kept on looking at his grandma. He might have, for the first time noticed the oldness of his grandmother as he looked at the wrinkles on her face that looked like an old road with lots of cracks in it. He then saw the black circles around both of her eyes, which might mean that she now hardly slept at night or she might have also been crying a lot, and he saw the white hair of his grandmother which now were whiter than they were earlier.

He loved this old friend of his, who stayed with him the most in the whole day when his parents were away for work. She meant a lot to him as she would always be there for him. She would play with him, get him dressed, make him eat with her own hands and tell him a new story every day. She was more like a parent for him.

Poor soul, trying to analyze the growing age of his grandmother at this small age, but if only he knew that, it all did not matter to her now and the only thing she might now be waiting for is her death, as this life hardly had anything left for her.

'Okay son,' she said, after thinking of a story for her cutie pie, 'Let us begin with our new story'

'Okay grandma,' said the boy.

Grandma began 'A long time ago . . .

30 YEARS EARLIER

(IN GRANDMA'S STORY)

A white Toyota Corolla, passed through the dark streets of Goa, at around 10:30pm.

She did not feel like a chirpy bride. All she knew was that, she has to serve her husband, do as told by her laws, go for her work and live like a simple bride. She could not think of love, nor for her husband, and nor for anyone else. Love no longer held any place in her life, for she married just for the sake of a change or may be because it is a part of life.

While Natasha did nothing, her husband, Ayush, sat next to her on the black seat of the car, wearing a white shervani and holding a pagdi in his hands (traditional Indian wedding wear for grooms) which he had removed just a while ago, was also in the same state as his wife Natasha was. He kept on staring outside the glass, looking at the empty street and some closed shops; with their names written on the top. Without uttering a word, he was lost in the memory of the things which changed his life, and which, he never thought will ever happen to him.

Both of them sat quietly, without talking to each other, and just gave a light and forceful smile when they unwillingly turned their faces and faced each other at the same time, just to not let the atmosphere be rude.

The driver would constantly look behihd, at the couple through the mirror in-front of him and then quickly get back his attention on the street so that the couples do not see him focusing more on them then on his driving.

They were perfect in every way. Ayush was a fair and handsome guy, with black spiked hair and had round black eyes, his skin was too white, making people think that he was not an Indian, and was a 5'9ft tall, twenty-nine year old man. Women were crazy about him when he was in college and at his work place.

Natasha, on the other hand, was a fair girl with long black hair. She did not look twenty-seven at all; people would consider her to be around 20 or a bit less. She had sharp eyebrows, white skin, a good height, and almost a zero size figure.

Both were well educated, allure and nicely brought up in an environment where they faced no trouble, but as it is always said, money does not mean everything in life. And so it was true in their case. Both were unlucky in love. God gave them one heartbreak after the other every time they fell in love. They had beauty and gorgeousness which attracted many to them, but only for the sake of fun, no-one ever showed them true love, but these two always opened out their hearts to who ever came into their lives, with the hope that they will someday find someone who shall never leave them.

They kept on waiting for love and eventually lost their hope in the end. They had no strength to love anymore and after overcoming all the heartbreaks and getting tired of family requests, they decided to get married.

————

Ayush and Natasha stood in lobby of Hotel Paradise, while their friends, brothers, and sisters went in a hotel room booked for these two, to make sure that it was perfectly festooned for Ayush and Natasha's first night.

They had just entered the hotel a few minutes ago and found themselves standing inside a big hall with white floor and a brown and red carpet over it, the ceiling of the hall was well designed with paintings of the various monuments of the world.

They stood in the reception lobby for about twenty minutes or so, without speaking anything or even looking at each other. Both of them would look elsewhere, either at the old paintings hanging on the walls, TV set in the lobby, people entering or leaving the hotel.

They were finally taken into their room after a long wait. Their room was completely bedecked with flowers.

There where flowers everywhere, on the bed, on the floor, and a few line of hanging flowers which dropped from top to each end of their bed. Lights were switched off, as there were candles placed all over the room, making it completely romantic and perfect for a first night.

All, other than Natasha and Ayush were preparing to leave, when, Tia a friend of Natasha came close to her and said,' don't worry sweetheart it will be fun, just don't sleep'. She then gave an impish smile to Natasha and left the room.

Natasha stood near the bed, while Ayush closed the door. They were both tensed, not knowing what to do. None of them spoke for a while, before Ayush broke the silence.

'I'll just freshen up,' said Ayush.

'Ya,' replied Natasha, as she saw Ayush going inside the washroom.

It never looked liked their first night. None of the two had any excitement in them, actually they hardly looked in the mood of getting naked and banging upon each other, and it was certain that their bed would be neat and tidy the next morning as it was at that time.

———

Natasha and Ayush first met about two months prior to their marriage at a coffee shop in Mumbai. Their parents, who were no longer willing to see their growing children stay single anymore or reach at the age where no one would agree to marry them, arranged the meeting.

They would still remember the day when they first met. Natasha had already reached the coffee shop by the time Ayush made there.

She was wearing a yellow salwar-kamizand she would look here and there all the time, while Ayush was dressed in a simple blue jeans and a black t-shirt. He would still remember seeing Natasha for the first time when he entered the cafe. She was sitting in the last table of the cafe near a big glass, where rays of the sun hit her straight. She seemed to be lost in some other world, as, she did not seem like she was actually waiting for someone. It was as if she had come there to be alone for some time with her own self.

Ayush then slowly reached her, and they started having the conversation with a usual 'Hi' and 'Hello'. They spoke about their work, or interests like every other first time meeting couple does, and sat there for about an hour or so, ofcourse, drinking more of coffee than talking.

Two days later they announced that they liked each other, and so, started the marriage preparation. The two did meet frequently but it never looked as if they were really happy. They met, sat together and talked on some topics but it looked as if they did it all forcefully. They never looked interested in any kind of talks.

They would give a light smile to each other whenever they sat side by side, and then turn around their faces and focus on their mobiles, hand nails, or newspaper.

There was no doubt that they did not love each other, but they did know that, if the other person came to know of the fact, than one will be shattered. And it would be wrong to make somebody else feel that, one married him/her just for the formality and not for love.

Wow, one would wonder what kind of a world is this. No love but still selflessness for each other. They never shared anything between nor was there anything in common between the two, accept one thing, and that was, a feeling, which knew that how would someone else feel if they knew that the person one has chosen as a life partner and the person with whom one has to spend the whole life with, and is expected to be supportive in all the goods and bads in one's life actually has no feeling for anybody.

The only thing they were oblivious of was that both shared this one common feeling and an experience which changed their lives forever, but which also brought them together.

"THERE ARE TWO KINDS OF PEOPLE IN THIS WORLD WHO MIGHT NEVER UNDERSTAND YOUR WORTH IN THEIR LIFE. FIRST ARE THE ONES WHO DO NOT LOVE YOU, AND SECOND ARE THOSE WHOM YOU HAVE LOVED AND CARED MORE THEN THEY DESERVED"

—PRATIK HINDOCHA

CHAPTER 2

Ayush slowly closed the door of the washroom, and headed straight to the washbasin. He opened the water tab and splashed some water on his face and took a towel hung right on a poll near the washbasin.

He kept on staring at the mirror above the wash-basin for a long time thinking of something or looking through the mirror at the white washroom which shone with the yellow light of the small lamps hung on the wall.He took a deep breath and turned his face to the right and closed his eyes for a while, may be because his mind was not yet happy. He wished he could avoid thinking of his past and get out of the mess he was in.

There was suddenly a buzz on his mobile phone which disturbed him from his thoughts. He then turned to where he had kept his phone and again took a deep breath before picking it up.

It was a message from a friend of his. He knew it would some funny message regarding his first night.

Ayush did not lift his phone from where it was, and instead he just pressed some switches and opened the message. He was right; it was indeed a message from his friend, which read like this;

"Ride like a horse who is never tired, have a nice night and JAGTE RAHO (stay awake)"

He gave a light smile to himself while looking at the mirror and locked the cell. He could not believe what was happening. Exactly two years ago, he was sending the same kind of messages to all his friends who were getting married and receiving replies from them. He would not mind receiving the same massage at that time, nor did he now, but it did not seem funny to him anymore. And the reason behind this change was Anamika, the girl who used to work with him two years ago.

Ayush, then, again turned to the mirror, as the thoughts of Anamika started running through his mind.

TWO YEARS AGO

(IN AYUSH'S THOUGHT)

It was a usual day at Saigal company office. People were seen leaving and entering the office through the huge glass door. The receptionist was busy on the phone and the clerks moved around with some files, in their silver colored uniforms-a shirt and pant.

The hall was the ground floor of a five storey building. It had a big fountain right in front of the entrance, across which was the reception table and three sofas kept in a semi-circle on the right hand side cross of the table, and the walls were filled with old paintings on every corner of the wall and had televisions hanged with only news channels on.

Ayush was sitting on the sofa near the reception table, working on a laptop when he first saw Anamika.

Anamika was fair, about five point two feet tall, and her lovely figure and curly brown hair just added to her beauty.

Ayush could not take his eyes off this beautiful lady in white shirt and black skirt, with glasses and with her hair slipped right till half of her back.

Anamika reached the reception table and said, 'Excuse me, hi, my name is Anamika Shah and I had an appointment with, Mr. Saigal at 10.00.'

'Just give me a moment,ma'am' said the receptionist, as she started going through the appointment list of her boss, and then made a call at her boss's(Mr.saigal's) cabin, before finely returning to Anamika, 'Mr. Saigal is busy in his meeting, so would you mind waiting for ten minutes?'

'Ya, it's totally cool' replied Anamika.

'Okay, thank you' replied the receptionist. By that time you can sit on the sofa, while I send something for you to drink'.

Ayush could not believe his eyes as he saw Anamika heading straight towards him and sitting in the sofa next to the sofa he sat on.

'God, she is so amazing,' Ayush said to himself, as he saw Anamika sitting next to him. She then took a magazine kept on the table in front of her and started going through it, while keeping her left leg on the top of her right leg, which made her left leg visible till her knees.

There was no way Ayush could have taken his eyes of Anamika who was smiling to herself as she went through the magazine. She looked completely stunning, especially with a smile on her face. Ayush could not do anything other than observing her beauty, her red lipstick, and a kind of pinkness in her cheeks, may be due to make up.

He would have hated the moment when the receptionist came to her, and asked her to go to Mr. Saigal's office on the fourth floor.

She was leaving already and Ayush was busy thinking what he should do. He wanted to see her all the time, he had never seen anyone so beautiful, he just felt like proposing her at that very moment, but he knew that it was a stupid idea. God, she was already waiting for the lift. Ayush was going mad, he did not know what happened, but he got up from his place, left his laptop and all his work where it was, and ran straight towards the lift. He needed to hurry, Anamika was already inside and the lift door was closing in. He thought he would not make to the lift, before Anamika pressed the open button, so that the lift did not close and Ayush could get in.

————

She was excited and nervous on her first meeting for her company. Anamika was so nervous thinking about it that she did not even notice when did the lift arrive, before another lady going inside the lift side-tracked her.

She still kept on thinking about the meeting as the door of the lift started to close in, but got disturbed again as she saw, a man in silver suit and pant, white shirt, and a dark brown tie, running hard to catch the lift. So, she hurriedly pressed the open button so that the man (Ayush) could come in.

'Hey, thanks,' Ayush said to Anamika.

'Its, okay,' replied Anamika,'Just a human duty'.

'Ya, true that I guess,' replied Ayush.

They stood next to each other. Ayush could feel her smell, which killed him. He kept on staring at this girl who was biting her own lips in nervousness, and looking up and down inside the lift.He surely hated the lift to move so quickly, as they reached the fourth floor.

They entered into the hall which had only one black door that was the office of company owner, Mr.Saigal. A three-seated sofa was kept on the right-hand side of the lift, and there was a silver and black table and chair right opposite to it, which was empty. And the rest of the hall was fully black in colour with just one big flower vase placed in a corner.

Natasha stood outside the black door, hoping that someone would come to call her. She was totally nervous till now, especially while she was inside the lift, when she noticed Ayush staring her. She wondered if there was a problem with her clothes, or was there something wrong with her face which is why this man stared at her.

Finally, a lady came out of the cabin and asked her to get in.

Ayush stood right there as Anamika went inside. He kept on thinking of her and the image of her first sight did not left his mind. He slowly headed towards the closed door and stood right a half foot away from it and touched the door with his hand, trying to feel the person who was on the other side of the door, he could not wait for the that face beautiful to come out and stand in front of him so that he could still admire more of her.

The door open after about thirty minutes and Anamika was finally out but with Mr. Saigal, Ayush's father.

'Ahh, meet my son,' Mr. Saigal said to Anamika.

'Guess I already have,' said Anamika as she looked at Ayush with an impish smile,' Just didn't know that he is the future boss of this company'.

'Ahh he is surely going to be a tough boss,' Mr. Saigal said, and then turned to Ayush, 'son, meet Anamika, daughter of Mr. Shah and your co-worker in our current project'.

Ayush could not believe his luck, the person who had become so close to him in last forty-five minutes as if they had known each other for a long time, would be with him for a long-long time now. He could not have been anymore happier than this. Ayush then controlled his thoughts, turned towards Anamika and said, 'Nice to meet you and I hope it will be fun working with you'.

'Same here,' replied Anamika.

'Okay, why don't you guys discuss regarding the project before it is time for Anamika to leave' said Mr. Saigal.

'Sure dad,' Ayush said and turned to Anamika, 'Shall we go to my office'.

'Why not?' Anamika said, with a smile on her face.

———

Natasha went near the bed, as Ayush closed the washroom door. She then held the big line of flowers falling from the top, where a nail in the ceiling hanged it. She admired them slowly by her hand as she moved from flower to flower, but then dropped on the bed with tears in her eyes. She sat on the bed, with her left hand on the bed to support, as it would have not been able to sit in a situation were she was emotionally weak.

'Why me? Why only me?' asked Anamika to god as she looked upwards.

As tears rolled out through her eyes, she too got lost in thoughts of her past.

TWO YEARS AGO

(IN NATASHA'S MEMORY)

'How can you do this to me?' Natasha asked.

Sidharth was busy packing his bag as both him and Natasha were returning back to Mumbai. They were in relationship for last one year but for Sidharth it was nothing more than just a fun time, he was never serious about it but he was surely aware that Natasha was, but, he never tried to have a talk with her about this. He wanted to have fun with her and it would have not been possible if he had told her that he wasn't serious about their relationship. Sidharth thought that she would cry for a while and eventually forget about it or even she might eventually start taking it as fun, but that didn't happen. And when Natasha asked him about their future after their first physical contact a night ago, Sidharth refused to marry her. He told her that he was never serious; it was all fun and told her that even she should not take it much seriously.

'Ohh, common man,' Sidharth said as he saw Natasha getting over emotional, 'Its all right, we can still be together but that doesn't mean we should marry and you can always have somebody else whenever you want to.'

'What? How can you even say that, I truly loved you?'

'Listen, don't be so old fashioned okay. How many people now a days are serious about each other and plus people do date and sleep together even if they do not marry, so, just chill.'

Sidharth then locked his bag, picked it up in one hand and his suit in another and started towards the door. As he reached near the door, he turned to Natasha and said, 'I have kept your tickets on the dressing table, in case you want to come, you can or your wish,' and he left, closing the door.

Natasha did not move, she sat on the bed covering her tearful face with her hands. She was totally broken. She was already dreaming of spending her life with the person she loved. She thought that she might be one of the luckiest girls with the happiest life, but it was all over now.

It was evening already; Natasha lied on the bed in her white and black nighty facing on her left side at the setting sun in the yellow sky. She was so happy exactly twenty-four hours ago. Sidharth had brought her inside this same room with her eyes closed and surprised her with candles all around the room and dinner on dining table with a bottle of champagne.

Her life was in heaven when Sidharth held her during their couple dance in the room after their dinner. She was wearing a black saree while Sidharth wore black pant and shirt.

She was totally lost in him. Natasha did not object when Sidharth took her to bed by lifting her in his arms. Natasha could smell his perfume and feel his tight chest as she kept on staring at Sidharth with her hands around his neck.

She was now on the bed. He slowly came near her and made his lips feel her cheeks and them slowly headed to her lips. They lied on the bed with their lips locked passionately; Sidharth kept his hand around Natasha's neck while she brought her hands around Sidharth's back and slowly moved them all over his back. Sidharth then brought out one of his hand and moved it to her stomach then slowly taking it on her back. He rubbed her back for a while before slowly opening out the strip of her blouse. This aroused both of them as they lost control. They kissed more passionately, as Natasha zipped him off, and Sidharth brought her saree down.

Sidharth then let his hand go inside her, as she jerked with no control over herself. She then started unbuttoning him and gave him kisses in his chest.

They lied on the bed with only a blanket covering them, and Sidharth moved his lips on Natasha's neck and shoulder.

'I love . . . I really love you.' Natasha said. Sidharth had by now totally lost his control, he was moving even faster than before, and he was enjoying her wetness. He then brought her breast near his chest and hugged her tightly, and gave her a big kiss on lips.

It was the best time for Natasha before she took the marriage topic and Sidharth refused.

She did not return to Mumbai, as she did not want to see Sidharth anymore. She had no friend in Goa. She would go on the beach, walk alone, sit in front of the setting sun and let tears roll out of her eyes.

———

Ayush was still in front of the mirror, he was out of his world but still glum. He then took a deep breath and let his hand slip in his right pocket. He brought out a condom packet. He looked at it, took a deep breath and let it go back inside his pocket.

'It's too late, I should go out so that Natasha will not have to wait,' Ayush thought.

Natasha was still sitting on the bed when she heard the door opening. Ayush was out in his night suit.

He headed to the table where he had kept his bag, as he saw Natasha entering inside the washroom.

Natasha was not able to control herself. She knew she would cry out but she did not want that to happen in front of Ayush, so, she went inside the washroom the moment Ayush was out.

Natasha sat on the edge of the tub crying her heart out in a low voice to make sure that Ayush does not find out of her emotions. She kept sobbing for minutes. She wished she had never fallen in love and had a heart which always dreamt of a prince charm.

On a day when a girl and boy feel like the happiest people on earth turned out to be saddest for this two. They did not know where the life was taking them, or was the decision they took right or not because no marriage life can ever work out if there is no love. It even might if there is something called love in one person, but the only problem here was that nor did Ayush or Natasha had love.

They were in tears, and they had a mind, which was filled with thoughts. They were now married people but none of the two wanted to think they were, because it will eventually bring back their old memories or fill them with the fear of hurting the person who had trusted them as life partner, or they may get divorced, though it won't hurt them that much but they were still in no mood of any break ups.

All they hoped and wished was, to let the things happen the way were. They made it in their mind to keep their pains within them only, and not allow any more trouble in their life.

> "LIFE ALWAYS GIVES US A REASON TO LOVE AND THAT LOVE EVENTUALY BECAMES A REASON TO LIVE."

PRATIK HINDOCHA

CHAPTER 3

Natasha sat on the bed with her cell phone in her hand and Ayush sat on the sofa with his laptop. It was turning out to be an interesting night. At the time when a normal couple would think of nothing else other then sex, these two were actually busy working. Ayush was busy correcting some of his documents, while Natasha chatted with some of her clients abroad through whatsapp. GOD, somebody help these people. One would actually wonder when was the last time they saw a porn film, it would have aroused them even if somebody had shown them an xxx clip just before they entered this room together. They seemed like a gay and a lesbo.

They did not even turn to look at each other, of course it would be wrong to say what were they thinking because they were not willing to fall in love and may be that's why there was no sex. But only if someone could explain them that there was nothing wrong in taking the erotic pleasure. It cannot certainly be boring if it was for the first time between different people.

Finally,after thirty minutes of silence, Ayush dared to look at Natasha and ask, 'Would you like to have something?

'Ahh,' Natasha said, not properly making out what Ayush just spoke and then corrected herself,' No, it's okay. I'm cool.'

'Well, I'm ordering a coffee for myself, thought you could use some too.' Ayush said, noticing the nervousness and shyness of Natasha.

'Okay. I think I'll have some,' Natasha said.

'Sure,' he replied with a faint smile.

He stretched his hand to reach the telephone kept next to the sofa, pressed the room service button.

He heard the first ring, and Anamika's image clicked in his mind.

Second ring.

Third ring.

Fourth ring. He rememembered the day when he saw her for the first time;entering the office buiding through the glass door.

Fifth ring. Somebody picked up the phone, it was a male voice. 'This is room service. How may I help you?'

'Hello, this is room number one-zero-one. I would like to know if I can get a coffee right now.'

'Sure sir,' answered a voice on the telephone,' Which one would it be sir, black or with milk.'

'Just hold for a second please,' Ayush said as he turned to ask Natasha which one she would have 'Would you like to have a black coffee or one with milk?'

'I will prefer with milk,' Natasha said.

'It will be two coffees with milk,' Ayush said on the phone.

'Okay, sir. It will reach your room in about fifteen minutes,' said the voice on phone.

Ayush kept the phone and returned to his work. 'I think she might be finding my behaviour bit strange', Ayush thought while he started at his laptop, but still gave no thought of having some chat with Natasha.

———

God, what I was thinking,Natasha thought. It was obvious for her to think like this. It really looked stupid when she first disagreed to his coffee offer and later agreed. It might seem as if she was confused or more like she was not comfortable. It might have looked rude, she thought again.

She could not concentrate on her work after, though she did continue focusing on her mobile phone but her mind was making her feel guilty about the stupidity she had just done.

She might be nervous because of my behavior,Ayush thought. It, was natural for him to think that way, and why not? Natasha was his wife, she was giving all her life to him and his family, and most important, this was their first night and instead of having any talk or not even trying to see if she was upset, so that he could comfort her, he started working.

Should I talk to her? I think I should, it would be better,he thought. So he stopped his typing work on the laptop, looked at Natasha and locked his lips, trying to find the courage to say something.

'Ahh,' Ayush spoke. He just uttered this and spoke nothing ahead.

'Yes. Did you say something?' asked Natasha. She heard him utter something, so she left her work and turned to him to ask if he said something to her.

'Nope. Nothing,' Ayush said. 'Just tired.' And focused back his attention on his laptop, doing nothing but still trying to show as if he was working.

'Oh, okay,' Natasha said.

Natasha felt sorry for him. She was already condemning herself for such behavior. She knew Ayush was trying to talk to her but was unable to and maybe it was due to her annoying behavior.

How stupid, Ayush thought. He might have gone mad to do it. Why did he even utter something if he did not have the courage to move ahead with the talk?

It was really amazing how both criticized themselves for the way they behaved. They knew, what they did was not right, but not even for a second did they realize that the other one is also behaving in the same manner.

May be this is what a heartbreak can do. They were not willing to talk, both were working on an occasion of which a normal person would dream of fun and both were lost in their own world. But the two still thought, that the other person might not find one's behavior to be good. It might make the other sad if one is in love because it's really excruciating when one is not loved back equally. They had many other thoughts in their head, but were unaware of the fact that both were facing the same situation. Both were sullen from within, had no faith in love, and might not love back anyone equally. They still cared for each other, even though they hardly knew anything about each other. They did not want the other person to be glum. They even thought that they made a mistake by agreeing to marry because eventually, it will only ruin their life if there is no love from one side, while there is tremendous from the other side. Though, to be true, there was no love from both the side but since they were unconscious of this fact, this is what they thought.

The doorbell rang twice. First, they thought, who could it be, but then they recollected that they had asked for coffee. It must surely be a waiter.

Ayush stopped Natasha, who, was getting up from her place to open the door. He asked her to sit down, while he stood and went near the door. He placed his left eye on the key hole to see who it was.

He saw a guy in white suit, white the hotel logo drawn on the left side of his chest. He stared at the door waiting for someone to open it. Ayush opened the door and allowed the waiter to come in. He asked the waiter to keep all the stuff on the table where he kept his laptop. The waiter quietly headed to the table, without saying a word. He looked left and right as he kept the tray, which, contained of milk, coffee, sugar, cups, and spoon on the table.

The waiter, was a bit nervous as he waited outside the door, as, he knew what were the people inside here for and he even guessed what might have they done or is doing or might be doing ahead. The thing he was worried of was that, in what condition he might see the couples.

He entered the room as the door opened. He first saw a man, who stood on the entrance in his black night suit and red slippers. He got inside and headed straight to the table to keep the coffee, as, he was asked to. On his way, he saw the young lady, or bride focusing on her mobile phone without looking anywhere, in her sleeveless white nighty, which was white in color, except for the part around her neck, which was black in color. Lucky groom, he thought as he saw the bride whose beauty was tantalizing.

No man, who saw her could have ever avoided her, but he was surprised to see the lucky man, who had all the right on her might just have not done anything, as, they had just come here as hour ago, and he saw a laptop on, which means they might be busy with something else. He was sure on his doubt when his eyes fell on the packed condom packet laid on the end corner of the white sofa.

The waiter than headed to the door after keeping the tray on the table and left as Ayush stood there while he kept the tray on the table, closed the door from behind.

Natasha then stood up from her place for the first time. She went near the table and sat on her knees. She then started to prepare the coffee by pouring the hot milk in the cup. Ayush, on seeing Natasha preparing the coffee went near her and said, 'you can sit on the sofa.'

'Ohh, ya.' Natasha said, and she stood up and sat on the sofa.

As she sat on the extreme right corner, her eyes felt on a condom packet laid next to her. She understood why was it here, but what she didn't understand was why wasn't it used? Ayush had started working but he might have planned it after he was done, but may be because she behaves strangely, is the reason why he did nothing.

Natasha, from the moment they had met, knew that Ayush was a kind of a quiet and shy person. May be that is why he did not move on due to her behavior, Natasha thought. She felt a bit bad for it. She wanted to have some words with him. She was trying to bring out courage and words so that she could start with something but before she could do that, Ayush started.

'So, you love your work ha?' Ayush asked.

'Well, yes. It just keeps me busy,' Natasha said, 'don't really prefer keeping myself free. It reminds me of my past so I just prefer staying busy.'

Ayush saw Natasha finishing the pouring of milk and lift the cup. She moved a cup straight to Ayush and gave it him. Ayush saw her eyes for the first time. First time in all this month, and could see them lost somewhere.

'Your eyes are just like mine,' he said.

Natasha stared at him as he said these words. They looked in each other's eyes and for the first time not unwillingly but with their own will. They spoke nothing for those seconds. For Natasha, it was for the first time in two years when someone might have actually tried to see her properly.

She too looked in his eyes. Was he in the same condition as she was in? she thought. May be not. May be it was because he was to kind and might have been thinking that she was upset. She did not wish to say anything, which would make them friendly. She was scared of getting involved in any relationship, even on knowing that she would be secured with Ayush. She had no courage to face any more emotional times as she had to. Her past always kept her in a fear of facing the bad time again. They were married but that did not mean that all will be fine forever.

'Don't think so,' she said. She kept her coffee on the table, stood up, and went inside the washroom.

It was nothing new for Ayush. He had seen people being worst to him, especially those for whom he had lots of love in his heart. He was trying not bringing out his tears but he was not able to control his thought.

(IN AYUSH'S THOUGHT)

More than two months had passed since Ayush and Anamika first met. They were working together all this time. They met every day, talked of their personal life, and went out for dinner or movies, etc.

Their friendship seemed to be moving to another level. Ayush knew that it was, but doubted that it might just be his own thoughts. There was no guarantee if Anamika too felt the same for him. He liked her and may be that is why he might be considering her friendship as her motivation to him, he thought. But he knew that, his thought did not matter. All that mattered was what Anamika thought for him.

He wanted to have her but that was not possible till the time he told Anamika about his feelings.

_____

It was Christmas of 2010. Every year the Saigal group organizes a big party for its staff at King's Palace hotel. Anyone who wished to have a private time with their family could have well skipped it, but hardly a few did that. Who would ever miss a huge party held it such big hotel, with all types of food for which one will have to spend have of the monthly salary they receive and they were allowed the access of a place which they only saw from outside.

The party hall was nicely decorated. It seemed more of a disco, with a DJ playing all types of songs, a bar with each and every type and quality of drink, LED lights shining the whole place, hundreds of balloons lying on the floor, names of the families written on the particular table reserved for them, people standing in their regular dress codes which was black shirt and pant with suit for males and white saree or dress for females.

Things were nicely placed. Ayush stood in a corner of the hall talking with some of his friends when his mobile vibrated. It was a message from Anamika, which said;

"WAITING FOR YOU IN THE MAIN LOBBY, COME SOON"

Ayush found this to be a bit strange. He left his glass on a table, and headed towards the door, passing by all the people who stood in the hall talking.

He climbed the stairs to reach the lobby on the ground floor. Ayush could not see Anamika, he looked here and there but still could not see her, before Anamika called him;

'Am right here.'

She was totally drunk. She stood near the lift on the far left corner of the lobby with a bottle of beer in her hand. Ayush knew she could create a mess in this situation, so, he ran to her and said,

'Okay, I think you had it too much today.'

'No, I didn't. I wanna have more.'

'Ya, but not today, right now I should drop you home.'

'Ooh come on, I wanna talk to you, that's why I called you out.'

And she gave him a naughty smile, kept her hands around his neck, and pressed the lift button.

'I don't really think you are in a state of talking right now.' He gave her a friendly smile.

The lift swung open, 'No. I think this is the best time,' and she got inside the lift pulling Ayush along.

She released one of her hand from his neck, pressed the button of top floor and got her hands back around his neck.

'Okay, now you are . . .'

'I am going mad,' she interrupted,' For you. I really want you.'

'Ya, but only after you are normal tomorrow.' she brought him more closer and said,' I am normal and I was normal on the first day we met when were staring me all the time.'

Ayush said nothing. He was surprised by the fact the that she knew, he was staring at her and she did not speak of it all this time.

'Weren't you staring at me?'

Ayush said nothing for a while, but knew that Anamika too felt something for him, something which he was not able to express. She looked pretty on that day and so did she at that moment. Ayush held her by her stomach, reached close to her lips, then, something stopped him. He went a little away from her lips, locked his eyes with her and said, 'Ya, I was. You looked so pretty.'

'I also do now,' she said.

They kept on staring at each other for a while. Anamika slowly lead her hand away from his neck and pressed the stop button. She did not want anyone to disturb that moment. They looked into each other's eyes and slowly moved their lips closer till they finally met and locked together.

Ayush could feel her tongue. He bit her lips and so did she, as they moved their hands on each other's back. It was something they were waiting for so long to happen. They were not going to apart very soon. They hugged more tightly and kissed more passionately. They were losing control but they knew that it wasn't the right place for moving ahead but they continued their act for some more time.

WHEN EVER YOU CRY

BILLIONS WILL SEE YOU

MILLIONS WILL COME AND SIT NEXT TO YOU

THOUSANDS WILL GIVE YOU WATER

HUNDREDS WILL CRACK JOKES TO MAKE YOU SMILE

TEN WILL GIVE AN ADVICE AND HUG YOU

BUT ONLY ONE WILL EVER DROP HIS TEARS FOR YOU

BECAUSE NO WONDER HOW LOW CONFIDENT THAT PERSON MAY BE

OR NO WONDER IF HE CANNOT CRACK JOKES AND MAKE YOU LAUGH,

BUT HE WOULD WISH THAT, THE ONE TEAR HE DROPPED FOR YOU, WOULD BE CONVERTED INTO THE SMILE OF YOUR FACE BY ALMIGHT.

KEEP THAT ONE PERSON AS LONG AS YOU CAN, BECAUSE PEOPLE WON'T DROP THEIR TEARS ON YOU FOR FREE. THEY DO THIS ONLY WHEN YOU MEAN SOMETHING TO THEM.

—PRATIK HINDOCHA

CHAPTER 4

She came inside the bathroom and locked the door. Tears started to roll out. She rested her back on the door and slowly slides down on the floor. The night was getting more emotional than she had imagined. It had been months since she had missed Sidharth so terribly.

It took her more than a year to overcome everything that happened between her and Sidharth. She was alone and depressed when he left her at the hotel. She spent around two weeks over there, alone and only answered the calls from her family. On returning, she sent a resignation letter at her office, without giving any strong reason for resigning but since her boss was more like a friend to her, she understood that something was wrong.

Natasha decided to change her working place because she knew that, if, she continued working there, she would have to see Sidharth every day and that was not possible. He did not love her and for the same reason she could no longer love him as well. It would have given her nothing but pain.

She left it all and went on a small holiday. She thought it would help her mind forget about everything that happened, but she was wrong. She thought of him the whole time and sleep seemed like a distant dream. She knew that, the more she would stay free and alone, the more she would think of him. So, she got herself a new job and took as much work as could, with the thought of ignoring her past.

This did help her a bit. She no longer thought of Sidharth as much as she used to, though he did cross her mind at least once or twice a day, but she was happy with the fact that his memories did not kill her from within as much as they used to.

Things were a bit better all this time, but all of a sudden, Sidharth was back in her mind. She feared of meeting the same doom again. It would not be as atrocious as the last time but she did not want to see any more trouble in her life, especially not another break-up.

Natasha splashed some water on her face, cleaned up with the napkin, looked into the mirror and thought, I should not have answered Ayush that way, it seemed really rude.

She then opened the door and went outside. Ayush was still sitting on the sofa, but this time, not working. His cup was on the table and he seemed to be lost somewhere else.

Natasha started walking to him slowly and hesitantly. She wanted to apologize to him for the rude answer she gave him a few minutes ago. She was feeling a little nervous about it but she knew that she had to do it. Ayush is her husband, he could have said her anything for the way she answered, but he said nothing.

She walked to the sofa and stood near Ayush, but he did not seem to have noticed her. He stared at the table, lost in his world, he did not even remember were he was or with whom he was.

'I'm sorry'.

Ayush was surprised by her words. This was hardly the second time she spoke something and that to a sorry.

'For what?'

'For the way I answered you a few minutes back.'

'Oh, that is fine. Am used to such type of answers. It does not feel bad, at least not anymore.'

He was right, Natasha thought. Their eyes did seem a bit similar. May be not just eyes but also their lives. She wanted to talk to him a bit more, not sure why, but she did wanted to.

'You too are a workaholic?'

'Just like you. Don't prefer being in the past.'

'May be your reason may not be as strong as mine.'

'Or, may be your reasons may not be as strong as mine,' Natasha gave out a small laughter, 'Hey, that is great.'

'What?'

'You actually even smile.'

'I smile every day.'

'Then where was it gone till today?' Natasha held her cup of the coffee with both hands and took a sip of it. 'Or, it gets lost somewhere whenever you see me?' Ayush said.

Natasha took a deep breath. This conversation reminded her of Sidharth. This was the same topic he picked when they first talked. Her heart was beginning to burden with those memories again, the memories she wanted to throw out of her heart. She was losing the interest of talking to her husband, but she knew that, it was for the first time since they have met that, they, seemed to be talking so freely, so, she decided to force herself into more on conversation, so that, it would at least develop a sense of approachability with the guy she has to live with.

(TWO YEARS AGO)

Natasha sat on a black leather seat next to Sidharth along with ten others in the conference hall.

'So, what do we do?' asked Sidharth, as he started to walk behind the chairs of people sitting on his left.

'May be we should close our sales,' said one of the employees, sitting four seats away from Natasha.

Sidharth stopped his slow walk, kept his hands on the chair of one of the employees and turned to the man who brought out such a stupid idea. But he knew that these types of answers were common and replying him back angrily or talking to him rudely won't do any good but that will surely reduce his morale and eventually effect his work and company.

'We began the production a year ago and such problems do occur when we have something new in the market.'

'Maybe we should advertise it more aggressively," said another employee.

'I don't really think that any other company advertises their products like we do.'

Everyone gave their own ideas, but none seemed satisfactory. Sidharth had already completed half a round and by now all seemed to have emptied their brains out. But Sidharth had his eyes on the young lady in white shirt and skirt, wearing black framed glasses, with a pencil in her mouth, and looking straight at the glass table without speaking a single word.

Sidharth slowly reached to her chair, kept his hands on it and said, 'Anything you have got for us, Miss Natasha?'

Natasha took the pencil of her teeth her, stood up and stood behind the main chair where Sidharth sat.

'Well,' she began,' we have done everything any best company in world can do, may it be advertising aggressively, giving away discounts, free gifts, etc.'

Sidharth waited for something to come of this young and definitely confident lady.

'But why don't we go to people.'

'What do you mean?' asked Sidharth.

'What I mean is, we go to people and ask why do they find hard to buy our product.'

Sidharth was expecting something much better from her but for a moment he thought that she has not done her homework properly. 'We have already done that, and only after going to the people did we launched our product.'

'Yes, we did,' Natasha continued, 'But, we last did it a month before launching our product, while our competitors are still doing the same. They do not advertise like we do nor do they provide as many schemes as we do.'

She took a deep breath.

"But they make sure that they are never out of touch with their customers. And so, what they do best, is talk—Talk to the audience and see the change in their taste and accordingly change their methods.'

'And that is now what we do?' asked Sidharth, lifting his hands from the black chair.

'Yes, that is what we do,' Natasha continued, 'We did every single thing any company would do to sell its product and much better than they did, but we still do not sell it as much as they do and that is because of this. We do not see what people want and what their affordability range is.'

'Well, we are in the market for years and people trust us, so it should not have been so hard for us to sell our product.'

"Over-confidence,' Natasha turned to face Sidharth,' this is our over confidence and as we all know. Over-confidence is never too good for health.'

Natasha again took a deep breath, turned her face from Sidharth and faced everyone.

'We sell to people, so we must know what they expect from us, and to do so, we must go to them and only then will they come to buy what we sell.'

No one spoke for a moment, then Sidharth brought his hands out of his pocket and started clapping her for a brilliant thought and his applaud was followed by the others.

'Well done,' he said, as he went near Natasha, still clapping his hands.

Everyone started to the leave the cabin one after the other. Sidharth preferred sitting on his chair as he kept on staring at beauty who just showed that girls can kick any damn stuff out.

It was not love. Though he did not take his eyes of Natasha, one thing, which remained true, was that he did not love her. He just had a thirst for her and he wanted to drink her out to end his thirst. He turned his chair backward, facing the big glass, which gave the clear view of the straight road, with buildings on both sides, and blue water at the end. I shall have her, he thought, while rotating a pen in his hand.

———

Six months had passed after that meeting. The idea that Natasha gave worked, but Sidharth was never able to have even one friendly word with Natasha, all the time they met she talked nothing accept work. Sidharth wondered if he would ever get a chance to have her, because seeing the way things were going, he wondered they would even become friends.

Sidharth was still busy thinking about him and Natasha at party held by his company in the hotel Pacifica, when he saw Natasha entering the party hall in her black and red saree, with sleeveless black blouse, wearing a simple silver chain in her neck and earring in her ears. She headed straight to him on floor of the huge white hall, which shined with different LED light. Passing through the other guests talking, standing alone with a glass of champagne or whine, Natasha took a glass of champagne from the tray of the waiter who crossed her in white shirt, and black pant and tie. She headed straight to Sidharth who sat on the big chair at the bar and stood right next to him without giving him any look. She turned her face to the right looking at her senior employee who had been staring at her from the moment she entered the hall.

'Congratulations,' she said, giving him a smile, 'Your hard work did bear fruits.'

Sidharth took a sip of his drink, kept it back on the table and faced Natasha.

'No, the credit is all yours. After all you are the one to have brought up this idea. You deserve your credit equally.'

'Well, may be.' She said, taking her drink and eyeing at Sidharth.

Sidharth kept his drink aside and looked at Natasha. 'What?" Natasha asked.

'Nothing, just wondering who could be the lucky man to have you,' Natasha brushed into laughter.

'You know what? You must be the thousandth guy to have asked me this.'

'And I must also be the thousandth guy to hear no-one.'

'Ya,' Natasha said, as she took another sip and emptied her glass.

'This is also strange.'

'What?'

'A serious lady who never smiled as if she were a principal of some school is actually laughing so much today.' Natasha could not have heard anything funnier than this. She was naughtiest among her group. Boredom was a word out of her dictionary and she did not have any school class without a new boyfriend.

'What? Give me a break. You never seen me smile does not mean that I keep like some old boring lady.'

'Well, I can see I was wrong.'

They looked into each other's eyes for a while, without saying a word, then Natasha gave him a light smile and asked, 'Are you checking me out?'

Sidharth went a step close to her and said, 'No, I am like . . . .'

He said his half sentence and left Natasha at bar. Suddenly, after heading a few steps, he turned back to her and said,' It seems like some good music to dance on.' They smiled to each other.

They stood on the dance floor. Ayush kept his hands around her waist and Natasha kept her hands around his neck. They were lost into each other as if they were long lost friends meeting after years. They could not see or hear anything else, not even the music nor the voice of the waiter who asked them to give him a bit of a space to pass. He saw the couple lost in another world, so he did not prefer to bring them back to reality.

They did not speak a word for minutes before Natasha broke the silence in her soft tone, 'You are like what?'

'I am like lost in you,' he took a soft breath, 'I am like lost . . . . in you.'

"DO NOT BE UPSET IF SOMEONE CALLS YOUR LOVE AND AFFECTION FOR THEM TO BE CRAZY OR STUPID BECAUSE SOME PEOPLE ARE JUST TOO BLIND TO SEE THE HIDDEN LOVE."

—*PRATIK HINDOCHA*

CHAPTER 5

Natasha turned to Ayush who smiled at her. She returned him a smile and said, 'Not really. It's just that. You know, get a bit nervous.'

'Ya. Nervous, happens to me as well.'

'I can see that. You never smiled before today.'

'Anyway, let's just keep this topic aside. We can have it some other time.'

'True. Am bored too.'

'What are your hobbies?' Ayush asked.

'Reading, drawing, playing piano, etc etc.' Natasha kept her coffee cup on the table and took a pillow and picked her coffee cup from the table.' What about you?'

He did not know what to say, so, he looked up for a second to think what were they, but all he could recollect were the ones Natasha had.

'Just the once you have. Reading, drawing, playing piano, etc and etc.' Natasha burst out into laughter. She did not remember when she did last laugh; obviously a normal person would smile a hundred times more than this in a day. But this much of laughter did meant a lot to a person who had forgotten the meaning of happiness since days.

'God, so, we do have something in common.'

'And we took months to know that.'

It was just getting better and better. Two people who seemed more like strangers a few minutes ago were finally able to bring something out, something which was common between the two, of course there still is a lot more common stuff to come but a beginning is always good.

Natasha stood from her place and went to the window. She slid the window glass to her left and allowed the air to enter the room. She first felt it on her cheeks, then on her hair and then its freshness was touching her whole body. She spread both her hands in front of the white moon in her nightgown and widely spread hair as if she was feeling some short of peace after many years.

Ayush stared at her. He did not know who was he seeing at that moment, a person who hardly spoke a word to him in all this time or a person who suddenly seemed to have become lively in last few moments as if she did not know the meaning of sadness and pain. But he was happy for whoever was in front of him. He gave a light smile as if he could feel what Natasha feeling, but slowly started to lose it as this moment reminded him of one more person who lit his house with her light and all of a sudden that small light turned into a big fire and burned his house of dreams.

(IN AYUSH'S THOUGHT)

Anamika stood in the beach sand in front of the dark water and setting sun, feeling the freshness all around her. It had been a few days since the night on that lift with Ayush. There was hardly a single day after that when they did not met or went for drive a night, had ice cream while they sat on the top of the their car or at a bench in the garden. Lunch was always together at their office or at a restaurant and being alone was always an excuse for kisses and hugs.

Ayush held Anamika's stomach from behind, gave her a kiss, and said, 'I love you.'

'I know,' she said with a smile, gave him a return kiss and continued. 'I love you too.'

They walked on the beach for a few minutes with the bottom of their lower wears held up to not get it wet and their sandals held in their hands. After a while, they sat in front of the sun which soon was gone only to nallow the darkness to take over the sky. Anamika rested her head on Ayush's shoulder and he kept his hand around her back.

'Thank you.' Ayush said. Anamika lifted her head from his shoulder.

'For what?' she asked.

'For being the part of my life, and making it so happy.'

Anamika gave him a smile and rested her head back over his shoulder. It couldn't have been any better. Two love birds sharing a happy moment together in front of the setting sun, and dark but beautiful water. It was all like a dream for Ayush but he was happy with it, only wishing that this dream never ended but he forgot that everything with a beginning has an end.

Natasha could feel the invincible touch of the invincible air all over her body, as she stood in-front of the open window in her white night wear. Her eyes were closed, and all her pain and sorrow seemed to have left her mind and heart at that time. She was living a new life for the past few seconds. She was completely lost, she had forgotten where she was, she forgot what bad had happened to her in the past, and everything that had crossed her mind in the last few hours. She smiled to herself, because her mind was at peace, she had overcome the trauma she had been through and was now feeling whole and complete.

Suddenly the wind started blowing, forcing her eyes open. All her peace and relaxation was now gone in a fraction of a second, and so was her smile. She knew where she was, she knew what all she had been through, she knew her life was a confusion, and most importantly, she knew that there was something that she wanted to forget but her heart was reluctant to let go of the strings.

(TWO YEARS AGO)

They sat on the top of car red HYUNDAI i10 front, parked a few yards from the edge of the green-grassy mountain. The sky was cloudy and dark. It was surely going to rain soon. There was grass on the land around the red car which moved due to the wind and trees too swayed as though dancing to the music of the wind. Even the slope of the mountain was covered with trees and grass.

Natasha lay on Sidharth who was lying on the car. He kept his hands around her neck and gave a kiss on her forehead.

Natasha smiled a bit, looked at Sidharth and said, 'I love you.'

'I know,' Sidharth said, 'and I can see that.' He gave another kiss on her forehead and said,' I love you too.' Natasha's hair blew all over her face due to the strong wind.

'Just don't leave me.'

'Oh, common. Why would I ever do that?'

Natasha looked at Sidharth and said, 'I know, but, it's just that, I find it so hard to trust.'

Sidharth turned his eyes on her, gave a smile, and said, 'So, you do not trust me haa?'

Natasha 's experience betrayed her trust and try as much she could not overcome her fears. She had a new boy-friend every year in her school and university. People considered her to be a slut, or someone who hardly gave a damn to anything or anyone and had no heart. She was hardly seen crying. Even after her break-ups, she would be seen chilling around with friends, partying, and looking for new guys.

Natasha got up and walked on the green grass with her hands folded, and stopped after walking a few steps. A drop of tear rolled through her eyes, flowing down her soft—smooth cheek, and finely dropping on the ground. 'I had a new boy-friend every year.'

'Wow, that's great,' Sidharth laughed out.

She turned to him with her wet eyes. 'Am not joking,' She said, with a low, sad voice, 'I was a fantasizer. Someone always lost in her own world,' she continued as she took slow steps to Sidharth (her hands no longer folded),' Like every normal girl, I too had a dream of having my own prince charming, I too dreamed of living a happy life with someone whom I love and someone who loved me back equally.'

Sidharth got on his foot as Natasha came closer to him.

'May be that is why. I always trusted all men who came in my life with an open heart and closed eyes. I thought, I had what I wanted. But in the end all I got was a broken heart.'

Sidharth put his arms around her and said, 'Do not worry it happens at this tender age.'

Natasha shed some more tears. 'I know it does, but about what after? Why was it so hard to find someone who gave me what I gave him?' She continued, 'I always kept a strong heart even after all this. People thought I was some sort of a slut, but, I wasn't. I too had a heart which cried every second of the day but I did not let anyone see it because I did not trust anyone, thinking that all are the same; willing to use me.'

'It's okay, things will be fine now.' Sidharth said tying to comfort her.

'You know,' she took a pause and continued,' all this time, I have been dying to share my feelings with someone, but, I was unable to.'

'But you are sharing it with me now, and that is because you trust me.'

She hugged Sidharth and said, "Ya I do"

———

She gazed out of the window at the full white moon. What game was her life playing with her? She thought. She then turned back to face the room and rested the palms of her hands on the edge of the window, and looked around. There was hardly any change in the room: the bed was as neat and tidy as it was earlier, the bags kept next to the wooden cupboard on the left hand side of the door, the room shining with the yellow light, the coffee cup and tray placed on the white table in-front of the black colored two sit sofa, and finely Ayush, who sat on his place and kept on staring at Natasha.

She gave him a smile and turned her gaze at the white floor, trying not to look at Ayush, maybe she felt nervous or may be because of the way things were going.

———

His eyes were fixed on her. Natasha looked prettier than ever before, Ayush thought, he would lost himself in her, but it was not to happen. Even this beautiful moment reminded him of his past.

(IN AYUSH'S THOUGHT)

Ayush opened his eyes on the white bed kept in-front of the wall with black coloured flower wall paper. His naked body covered with only a red blanket. He lifted his upper body a little bit and rested both his hands on the bed, as he looked at the with door in the middle of black walls in-front of him, with two big brown vas kept on each sides. He slowly turned to his right at the curve shaped white dressing table in the corner and looked at his shirtless upper body in the mirror. He then turned at the extreme right to find

Anamika standing in-front of the open window and looking at the bright morning sun in her black nighty.

Ayush took the blanket off him and wore his jeans lying next to the bed. He walked towards Anamika and stood behind her, kept his hands around her stomach and kissed her cheek.

'Good morning,' he said.

'Good morning,' she replied with a smile, turned around and continued, 'shall we go for break-fast?'

'Okay, at your favourite place.'

They headed to hotel "Piri-Piri', near Juhu beach in a black Scorpio. Ayush was handsomely dressed: blue jeans—black shirt—and black goggles; and Anamika looked stunning: white sleeveless top—and a cream three-fourth—and black goggles.

'Happy now?' Natasha asked.

'Yes, very.'

Things were not going fine between them since last few weeks. Anamika was getting too busy with her work due to which she hardly gave much of her time to Ayush, while, Ayush on the other hand wanted to spend most of his time with her. There was never any work which stopped Ayush from meeting her. So, what if Anamika wasn't free, Ayush would leave any of his work when-ever Anamika needed him or he came to know that Anamika was free and they can have a time together; to chat, go out somewhere and be alone. But lately, things were getting worst. Anamika seemed more interested in her work than Ayush. Their relationship, hardly seem to mean anything to her, at-least, when compared to her work.

This made Ayush more insecure and worried. He started feeling that their relationship was coming to an end; they hardly spent time together, talked only a few times in a week, and saw each-other through the cabin glasses or in meetings. Ayush would run behind Anamika to talk on this matter but all she would say is, "It's all fine, nothing is wrong between us. Stop thinking such things".

She was not worried, but Ayush was, and he knew that their relation was not as fine and smooth as Anamika thought it to be, and he knew that the only solution to this was to have a heart to heart talk.

Ayush reached her apartment a night earlier (before this day when they are heading to the restaurant); worried, tensed and in a mood which lacked hue and lustre. They had an hour long talk. Anamika kept on convincing him that "All was fine between them, it was just because of the current work load that they were not able to spend enough time together but it will all be fine in a few weeks and he was putting an extra stress on himself by thinking so much".

It took a bit of a time before Ayush was convinced after which they had a romantic candle light dinner at her place and then made love all night.

They reached hotel "Piri-Piri" and sat right in the middle of the crowd. Ayush ordered his break-fast: toasted-cheese sandwich and black tea. And Anamika ordered for her light break-fast: an omelette and a green tea.

'Listen. I' am really sorry,' said Anamika.

A waiter paced by their table holding a white tray.

'It's okay,' Ayush said, 'doesn't matter.'

'I know it does, but, you know . . . Things are not too fine and that is the reason why I keep so busy and that's the only reason why I am not able to give my time to you . . .'

A waiter came in and kept a tray containing tea and coffee. 'Thank you,' Ayush said, looking at the waiter.

Anamika continued, 'But it does not mean that I do not love you, in-fact I think of you all the time.'

Ayush took a deep breath, turned his face to the left at the beach and looked at the people, some walking on the sand, some selling colourful balloons or eatables, children playing in the sand or taking bath in the water, and few jogging in their sportswear.

He then turned back his attention to Anamika and said, 'It's really okay. You know I do not ask anything from you, anything at all . . . except for your love and you telling me that you love me and that you too think of me while working, is hell enough for me.' He held her hands on table and gave her a smile.

'Thank you,' Anamika said.

'No need to,' he continued 'you know, I had fallen in love with you from the very first moment I saw you . . . when you got inside the office on that day and the only thing I wished for, at that time when you were in-front of me was you . . .'

A waiter came in again with their break-fast and said, 'A cheese-toast sandwich for sir and an Omelette for madam,'.

Ayush continued, 'I ask you nothing, nothing at all except for your love.' He took another deep breath and continued, 'you know I have had many girls coming into my life and going away, as if, I was a toy. They played with me as long as they wanted to and left. I am not saying I did not love them. I actually did and definitely had feelings for them and it really used to hurt me when they left, but, the feeling which I have for you is the one which I did not have for anybody else and I do not wish to part from you. All I ask for, is, stay with me and keep loving me just as I love you.'

Anamika kept her left hand on top of Ayush's hand which holded her opposite hand and said, 'I'll never leave . . . promise and I'll always keep on loving you.'

Ayush felt so better by those last words of her, he could not have asked for anything more, except for having someone who would keep on loving him all his life.

He gave out a satisfied smile and said, 'Ah!!! Am hungry now, so, let's eat.'

The life was, at that time, taking a sublime turn for Ayush. All his worries and tension of his relationship with Anamika left him at that moment. He could not have thought of any more trouble, and the thought of having someone to understand him by his side made his world all more sublime.

"REMEMBER THAT THE MOMENT YOU THINK THAT YOU DO NOT CARE OF YOUR OWN TIME FOR SOMEONE, WHEN YOU MAKE YOURSELF AVAILBLE FOR SOMEONE, NO WONDER HOW MUCH SO EVER BUSY YOU ARE, IS THE TIME YOU HAVE FALLEN IN LOVE AND THE ONLY THING WHICH WILL HURT YOU AT THAT TIME WOULD BE THE MOMENT WHEN YOU LEARN THAT THE PERSON WHOM YOU LOVED, CARES ABOUT HIS OWN TIME MORE THAN YOU, because when you really love someone, you don't see your own time but you wait for the time when that someone comes to you."

—PRATIK HINDOCHA

CHAPTER 6

Natasha reached Ayush who sat on sofa, motionless, and lost in thoughts. She kept her hands on his shoulders and shook it a bit.

'Are you alright?' she asked.

Ayush was still lost in Anamika's thoughts when he was side-tracked by the shake of his shoulder by a hand. For a moment, he even forgot where he was and that there was only one person in that room who could have shaken his shoulders, but, it did not take him more than a second to remember all this.

'Yes, am fine, it's just . . . . ,' he paused. Not knowing what to say.

'Okay, I just wondered what's wrong seeing you motionless.'

'Ah! It's just nothing, happens with me a lot especially when I think too much,' the silence of the room ended due to the voice of a police siren of a passing police car. 'But do not worry. Guess we would be staying together for the whole life so you will slowly get to know me.'

Natasha gave a smile and said, 'True, and you will know me to.'

'Yes, I guess so,' he said. 'I guess it is an important thing for two peoples, who are to live together that they know each other very well.'

'Do you snore at night?' Natasha asked.

'What?' Ayush was surprised to listen this.

'I asked if you snore at night.' Natasha said, 'you said two people living together must know each other, so I just thought if you could let me know that, how much of my sleep will be disturbed at night?'

Both laughed.

'Ah! Am not really sure of this, but I have been told a few times that I do snore a little bit but not much, so, am sure you won't have to face much trouble in these case.'

'Ohh! That's better then. Okay now your turn.'

'Sure mam. So, how much time do you take to dress up for a party?'

'Okay, now this is really . . .'

Ayush interrupted, 'It isn't stupid. I must know how much late would, I be getting for the parties from now on.'

Natasha smile, she kept the second finger of her left hand in her mouth and continued, 'Not much, to be frank. Hardly thirty minutes.'

'Ohh, that's not much. Guess I' am one of the rarest lucky husband.'

Is this a new beginning? Who knows, may be yes. They are beginning to know each-other or at-least trying to know each other. May be it's the start of a small friendship. Where will it lead, nobody knows, but they at-least gave a start to their relationship. It is said that we can only spend our life with the person whom we know and not with the one whose life is a mystery to us. So what if they might be talking forcefully right now, but they would at-least get to know each-other a bit better, and who knows, they might know of each-other more than anyone else does.

Anamika's image ran through Ayush's mind, but he was sure that, he did not want to stop the chat with Natasha, because he was not sure if Anamika's image will ever leave his mind or not, but, he did know that Natasha was one person who shall always be with him in the rest of the journey of his life and to pass out that journey even a bit happily or while keeping Natasha happy, it was necessary for him to know her, and this, he thought, was his best chance and a start, and plus, he seemed to be enjoying their chat.

'Okay,' Ayush said, 'now, let us discuss some basic things, like favourite food, movie and etc.'

'Sure, sounds fun,' Natasha said.

'Okay, so, I'll speak the word like food, game, movie and etc. You will answer first and then me,' Ayush took a deep breath, while they heard the sound of another siren. 'Okay, let's start. First, what is favourite movie, English and Hindi?'

'Well, it's "EAT, PRAT AND LOVE" for English, and, Ahh! "DDLJ" for Hindi.'

'That's great. And me for its "A-team" for English, and "DDLJ" for Hindi.'

'Oh! My gosh, so we do have some more thing in common.' They laughed.

'Well, you can call it our luck that we have things in common and it is only today that we know about it. Anyway, let's move to the next, favourite food?'

'It's "PAV-BHAJI" and "PANI-PURI". Now, please do not copy me.' She smiled.

'Am sorry to say, Miss. Natasha, but this are my favourite dishes to.'

'Okay, now before I start thinking that you are lying let me ask the next one, favourite actor and actress? From the earlier movies and new ones.'

There was a buzz on Natasha's phone of a whatsapp massage, and two more after a second.

'Okay, so, in actors it's "Big B" from the earlier movies and "Akshay Kumar" from the new ones. And in actresses it's "Sri-Devi" and "Katrina", and yours?'

'Guess we have similarities here too,' another buzz of the massage. 'Except one, I will like to add "Madhuri" in the place of "Sri-Devi".'

Few more buzzes of mobile.

'This is really disturbing,' Natasha said. She stood-up to switch her mobile off. As she headed towards the bed to switch off her phone, Sidharth's image struck her mind. She picked her phone and switched it off, with the memory of the day Sidharth left her in the hotel and ended their relation, also destroying her completely from within.

'Its fine now,' she said, as she headed back to Ayush. 'No more disturbance.'

'So, did you also chat with your friends on their first night?' Ayush asked. He took the final sip of his coffee.

'Oh! No,' she said in a surprised voice, 'it wasn't a friend. A client. She is in US, and does not know of my marriage.' Ayush gave away a small laughter.

'Okay. So, let us begin.' Natasha sat next to him.

'Favourite sport?' she asked.

'Cricket.'

Ayush went on to take another sip of coffee, not aware that he had already finished it.

'Good . . . my sir, same here.' Anamika said, bowing down her head a bit, with a hand slightly below her neck and a friendly smile on the face. 'Now . . .'

'Wait,' Ayush interrupted, 'Am done with my coffee. Wanna have another one, you interested?'

'At this time?' she asked. In a shocking voice. 'You think they'll be open?'

'Ofcourse they will be. We don't pay seven-thousand for a half day service.'

'Okay then. Make the coffee with milk again.'

'I-I captain.'

Ayush turned to the phone on his left and dialled the room-service number. It rang the first time. Ayush looked at clock which showed 1:30 am. Anamika's image struck his mind, when he first saw her in white shirt and black skirt.

Second ring.

He could imagine her smiling at him right now or no . . . Maybe it is laughter, stating him a fool to have ever trusted her and still expecting her even while knowing that she won't give a damn to him. He might already be history or a death present for her. But, inspite of all this, she is his present.

Third ring.

He could feel her mocking him for ruining his life for her and for being such a serious damn, trusting her for everything and what she ever said to him.

Fourth ring. He heard a voice. Someone finely picked up.

'Very good-evening sir. How may I help you?' The voice asked. It was a female voice; soft, gentle and kind.

'Yes, ah . . . this room is number "one-zero-one" can you please send us two coffees with milk'

'Sure sir,' the lady answering the call looked at the watch; round and black. 'It will be at your room in less than ten minutes.'

'Thank you so much. That's very kind of you.' Ayush said. He hung up.

———

Natasha stood in-front of the window looked at moon in the dark night. Biting her lips. He (Sidharth) crossed her mind again. The same image of him closing the door and leaving her alone forever kept on rewinding inside her mind.

She could hear Ayush talking to room-service staff on the phone.

Sidharth had drifted from her mind. She was enjoying the beauty of the moon, but only for a moment. Sidharth was back again in few seconds. She didn't know what was happening to her. She was confused, worried. She was feeling good talking to Ayush, but then, this pause reminded her of the first person she would want to forget and the last person she would ever want to meet.

Ayush slowly tapped her shoulders and asked, 'What happen? Looks like you really have a habit of getting lost like me.'

'I told you that,' she said (smiling). They were back, sitting on the sofa.

'Okay. We can now move ahead.'

'With what?' Natasha asked with a surprised look on her face.

Ayush returned her the same surprised look.

'Oh!!!! Yes,' she said. Finely recollecting what were they doing. 'Am sorry. Almost forgot. Okay, so, favourite book?'

'"THE LOST SYMBOL" by Dan Brown.' Natasha laughed with both her hands covering her mouth. 'What's so funny?'

'"THA DA VINCI CODE" by Dan Brown.' Natasha said.

'So that's funny. We're both fan of thrillers and same author.'

'Right.'

The doorbell rang. 'Must be our coffee,' Ayush said, as he stood up to open the door.

He looked through the key hole. He was the same guy who had come to give their coffee earlier. Ayush opened the door and allowed him to get inside.

'Don't you sleep young man?' he asked the waiter.

'Not really sir . . .' He kept the tray and the table, 'but it is already a habit so no problem.'

'So, Ayush?' Natasha spoke, 'What's your favourite holiday spot?' the waiter picked up the earlier cups and trays.

'Wow! That is surely an easy question . . .' The waiter headed towards the door to leave. 'Home'. Ayush closed the door as the waiter left.

'Ohh!! Common,' Natasha said, 'That's not a destination.'

'It is, for me . . .' Ayush started towards Natasha. 'That's what I like doing, spending time at home during holidays, lying the whole day on sofa and watching T.V.'

'Common, even I like doing that but there must be a place other than home you be going to or willing to go to; a city or a country?' Ayush took his cup of coffee and headed straight to the white bed decorated with flowers and sat on the floor supporting his back with the bed.

'Let me think then.' He sipped his coffee and continued, 'Venice, the most exotic place in the whole world.'

'Yap, and the most romantic of all, and un-fortunately . . .' she picked her cup of coffee and spoke, 'my favourite too.'

———

The waiter stood outside room number 101 with the coffee for the newly wedded couple second time on that night. He was another person as confused as the couple inside the room on that night. He did go in the rooms of newly married couples earlier as well but that was only for the purpose of cleaning after they had left. He was nervous of what he would he be seeing when he gets inside.

He rang the door bell.

He had just been inside the room about an hour ago, though he did not saw anything or felt anything which he should have actually felt in the room the couples spending their first night, and nor was he expecting to happen ahead, but, he still felt nervous with the thought that nothing can be said of any situation.

The door opened while was still busy thinking. He Saw Ayush opening the door as he did the last time.

'Don't you sleep young man?' Ayush asked.

The waiter headed to keep the tray on the table and saw the bride sitting on the sofa. He could tell by her expression that she looked more comfortable now than she did an hour ago.

'Not really sir . . .' He kept the tray and the table, 'but it is already a habit so no problem.'

'So, Ayush?' Natasha spoke, 'What's your favourite holiday spot?' the waiter picked up the earlier cups and trays.

As he started picking up the stuffs he had bought earlier, he took a gaze at the bride who seemed to have turned much prettier in last hour. He was becoming more jealous of the man who was lucky enough to have received such a beautiful treasure.

He picked up all things and headed to the door.

'Wow! That is surely an easy question . . .' Ayush spoke.

He left the room and, "Home" was the last word he heard, from Ayush.

He headed to the lift, confused, about what was happening inside the room, and with the longing desire for the bride's beauty who, he knew, will never be his.

———

'So . . . did you have a girl-friend?' Natasha asked. Her back rested on the sofa and eyes fixed on Ayush.

Ayush began in a soft and innocent voice, 'Ah! Yes. I did and I won't lie to you.' he looked up at ceiling in thought and got back his eyes on Natasha, and continued, 'not really sure how to begin.' He took another pause and started, 'many, and am a lot sure that, or maybe, I did fall for them seriously. I would have loved them to be a part of my life forever but, guess, I was unlucky . . .' he gave a glum look to

Natasha, took a deep breath and continued, 'but you know what . . . maybe they were never to be a part of my life, because I did cry, and cried a lot but, eventually, after a week or two, things would get back to normal and I would move on. But to be frank I did became sad all the time, and especially because I was a short of a day dreamer who would always dream of a future with girl I will be with.'

Natasha kept her eyes fixed on Ayush; her back no longer resting on the sofa and her cup of coffee in hand.

'You know . . . your story is just like mine.' She closed her lips, took his eyes of Ayush, looked down on the floor (trying not to get emotional), and brought back her gaze on Ayush. 'I too have been through this situation when I ever fell for someone. It made me really scared. I used to wonder if this could be the only meaning of love; heart-breaks, tears, loneliness and memories of someone who won't even give a damn about you.' Ayush looked at her with the eyes of sympathy as Natasha turned her face to her left and got back to him after a few seconds. She continued, 'then I don't want it. Why should I ever have something which gives me only pain and loneliness?'

They spoke nothing for minutes. They knew how similar their life was and they were unaware of it till now. They still are. They do not know that there still is a thing, which is still hurting them so much, which still is a part of their life at the moment.

This was the first time in last few months they met that they are able to talk so freely, bring out whatever they wanted to (not yet completely though), know each other and felt a bit comfortable together. They do not know if the same moments will continue for life long or for years or days, but they were enjoying this small moment together. True, there was a pain and an old memory even at that moment, but, it seems to have lessened as they get busy listening to one another.

"THERE IS NO AMAZING MOMENT THAN THE ONE WHEN YOU ARE WITH THE PERSON YOU HAVE ALWAYS WANTED TO BE WITH AND DID ALL THE THINGS YOU HAVE DAY-DREAMED OF; HAVING A PERSONAL MOMENT, SITING ON THE LAPS OF YOUR BOYFRIEND WHO KEPT HIS ARMS AROUND YOU, SHARING EVERY SPECIAL THING, HAVING SOMEONE WHOSE ONE LOOK MADE YOU FEEL SO GOOD AND MOST IMPORTANTLY . . . HAVING SOMEONE WHO LOVED YOU BACK EQUALLY EVERY MOMENT OF YOUR LIFE . . . HOW AMAZING WOULD IT BE? JUST THINK."

—PRATIK HINDOCHA

CHAPTER 7

The clock ticked 2:00 am. A silence took over the room. Ayush and Natasha spoke no words for the past few minutes. Their cups lied half empty.

Ayush stood at window with his hands rested on the edge. He saw no stars in the pitch black sky. He could see, just the moon, bright moon. He then moved his attention to the road down the hotel, followed by beach sand and then water for miles.

The road was deserted, just two or three beggars sleeping on the footpath, opposite right end of the hotel. There were street lamps, not strong enough to brighten the whole street. A car passes by, coming from his left and moving to his right. Two more comes from the same direction, and then comes a bike from the opposite direction; right to left. Might be some rich jerks, he thought, the cars and bike these days is more of a status symbol than a thing of necessity.

He took his hands off the window's edge and closed the window glass. He turned his face around and faced Natasha, who had the palms of her left hand on her cheeks and hers eyes fixed on the table. Without saying a word, he headed to the bed. His eyes felt on the flowers which lied on the bed. They were no longer too fresh. He then sat on the floor like earlier, picked up his cup of coffee and took a sip from it.

'It's beautiful isn't it?' Ayush asked Natasha.

———

There was no exchange of words between Natasha and Ayush. Natasha's mind was clear (from any thoughts). She looked here and there, and then at Ayush, who stood up and went to the window.

She kept on staring at him for minutes before her mind took her to the place she never wanted to go; in her memories.

(IN NATASHA'S THOUGHT)

Sidharth stood in-front of the window, staring at the beauty of the beach in-front of their resort. It was a sunny day, with white sands and completely blue water. Sidharth wore a white shirt and black jeans.

Natasha entered the room; in red sleeveless top and white pant. She kept her purse on the wooden table on the left side of the door and walked through the bed with white sheet and black blanket. She stood opposite Sidharth at the other end of the glass window and gave him a romantic and a satisfied smile.

'What?' Sidharth asked, with a return smile.

Natasha turned her face to see the amazing view. 'We finely have our own personal time after a year.' She turned to face Sidharth.' I was waiting for this . . . for being with you alone, with no work or any other disturbance, so, that we can have a better time to know each other.' she moved closer to Sidharth and continued, 'and not face any trouble in our future together.'

Sidharth kept his arms around her and said, 'Me too. I was also waiting for this time with you,' "but not for the same reason as yours", he thought. 'We'll have great time together.'

'Ya,' she smiled, 'we will.'

Her phone rang.

'Oops!! Guess we already have a disturbance,' Sidharth said.

Natasha brought out a small laughter and said in a soft voice, 'Don't worry, it won't happen a lot.'

Sidharth let Natasha free from his arms. She went to the wooden table, brought out her mobile phone of her purse and left the room while talking.

Sidharth turned back his face towards the beach and in thoughts. He was excited as well, but, his excitement was more and short lasting than Natasha's. He was never in love with her. All he had was a thirst for her body and he knew that this was the perfect opportunity for him to fulfil his desire and do what he had always been dreaming to do with Natasha, but, he knew he would have to be careful and a bit slow because he did not want Natasha to know what was going on at the back of his mind. And, so what if she got to know of it later, eventually, she would forget everything and move on with her life, he thought.

He closed the windows and drew the curtain.

———

Natasha was still lost in hers thought; her cheek rested on the left hand palm and eyes fixed on the table. She was vexed by what Ayush had said. Since she was too busy in her own world, she could not get what he meant.

'Sorry! Come again.' She said.

'I said, the silence isn't it, amazing?'

'Oh! Yes, it surely is.' She replied softly.

'So, why didn't you marry till now?' Ayush asked, 'I mean, why you waited for such a long time?'

'Uuf! Well, never found a good guy . . .' she paused to search for better answer. She thought for few more seconds and continued, 'you know, one may not necessarily find someone who would love one back equally or more than anybody else, and, as I had told you, I have always been unlucky in love, so, this is the reason.'

'Oh, ya, just like me.'

'And what about you, what took you so long?' Natasha asked.

Ayush gave a thoughtful look and spoke, 'Just like you. Never found someone who would have loved to keep her ass tight on me.'

'Hahahaha.' Natasha laughed, 'nicely said. Wow! I didn't know you could answer this way to.'

Ayush gave her a friendly and said, 'you ain't know lot of things about me yet, but do not worry, I give such answers does not mean am a bad boy.'

'Not at all', still laughing, 'I am not thinking that way at all, in-fact, I do like such guys, you know . . . who would just say out the first word that comes in their mind.'

'Great. Cheers to that,' he raised his cup of coffee and Natasha followed. Ayush continued, 'that means you're same, just like me.'

'We shall know that,' she said; smiling and her left hand rested on sofa.

⬚✛🖐︎🖐︎☠ ❄️🖐︎🖐︎ ✌️☼🖐︎🖐︎ 🖐︎🖐︎ ✌️☼🖐︎🖐︎🖐︎🖐︎

❄️🖐︎🖐︎ ✛🖐︎☼☹🖐︎ 🖐︎🖐︎ 🖐︎☼🖐︎✝🖐︎🖐︎🖐︎🖐︎

✝ ✛🖐︎❄️🖐︎ ❄️🖐︎🖐︎ ✝🖐︎🖐︎☺🖐︎ 🖐︎🖐︎ ☹🖐︎✝🖐︎🖐︎

🖐︎✝❄️ 🖐︎❄️ 🖐︎🖐︎ ☠🖐︎🖐︎ 🖐︎🖐︎❄️🖐︎🖐︎☆ 🖐︎✝☼

✌️☼🖐︎🖐︎ 🖐︎🖐︎☼ 🖐︎ 🖐︎🖐︎🖐︎ ❄️🖐︎🖐︎❄️🖐︎🖐︎ 🖐︎🖐︎

✛🖐︎ 🖐︎🖐︎☼🖐︎🖐︎🖐︎ ❄️🖐︎🖐︎ 🖐︎🖐︎☼❄️🖐︎🖐︎☠🖐︎🖐︎☼ ☎️🖐︎✝☼

🖐︎✝🖐︎☹ 🖐︎🖐︎☠🖐︎🖐︎ ❄️🖐︎ 🖐︎🖐︎🖐︎ 🖐︎🖐︎ ✛🖐︎❄️🖐︎

❄️🖐︎🖐︎ 🖐︎🖐︎✌️☼❄️🖐︎☠🖐︎ 🖐︎☼ 🖐︎🖐︎❄️☼🖐︎🖐︎🖐︎⬚

"WHEN THE GREAT GOD CREATED THIS WORLD, HE PROVIDED US WITH THE VODKA OF LOVE, BUT IT DID NOT SATISFY OUR GREED FOR A GOOD TASTE, SO WE FORCED THE BARTENDER (OUR EVIL MIND) TO MIX IT WITH A DRY VERMOUTH OF HATRED."

—*PRATIK HINDOCHA*

CHAPTER 8

(BACK TO PRESENT WITH GRANDMA IN THE GARDEN)

'. . . and it seemed like they were finely enjoying together . . .'

'Grandma . . .' interrupted the boy, 'am bored with this story, don't you have some fairytale for me today?'

The old lady did not know what to say. She had a lot of things in her mind but at that moment, when she was too busy in the story closed to her heart, she did not have emotions to speak of anything else.

'Oh! No my boy, your grandma does not have anything else for you today.' She said, in a low voice, feeling unhappy that she had to upset her boy.

'That's okay grandma.' Said the boy in a soft tone, 'we can have it next time . . . can I go and play with my friends if you don't mind.'

'Oh!! No my boy why would I mind that. Go and enjoy yourself.' She said, in a low voice.

'Thank you grandma,' the boy got up and ran towards the other kids.

The old lady lifted her face to the sun. She suddenly heard her grandson's voice.

'Grandma,' He shouted.

'What is it my boy?' she asked.

He came back running to her and said, 'I love you,' and gave her a gentle kiss on her cheeks with his soft lips.

The old lady was over-burdened with emotions and she replied, 'I love you too my child . . . now go and have fun.'

She saw her grandson running to play with the other kids in the sandy area of the park. She forgot all her pain for a moment. She kept her eyes on her grandson and got lost in his play, as if it were the only thing which made her happy and she ever wanted to see.

'Natasha . . .' came a voice from somewhere in the garden. The old lady (Natasha) was vexed, looking at her grandson as she looked around for the person who called her.

She looked at her left but saw no one except few people standing in rows, performing yoga and a few people walking on the track.

'Natasha . . .' the voice came again. It was familiar. She looked to her right this time, trying to see who it was, looking for an old familiar face. Still she saw nothing except children swinging or climbing trees. She turned behind but saw only green trees.

'Natasha am here,' the voice came again. Natasha was sure it (the voice) came from her left. She might have missed the person as she looked here and there in a hurry and surprise.

She was right; it was her old friend, Tia (her friend who advised her on the first night). It had been almost ten years since the two had met. Tia had shifted to Canada after her son settled there. They were planning to stay in India, but it gave no happiness to Tia and her husband in staying alone and miles away from their only son, so in the end they decided to move with him in Canada.

She stood behind the people standing in row, waving her hand to Natasha. Natasha waved her back with smile on her face.

Tia walked through the row of standing people and went straight to Natasha. Natasha could see that her old friend to had grown old, she had long white hairs, with no wrinkle around her eyes and dry skin. She wore a silver t-shirt and black track.

'Hi!!' Tia said. She hugged her the moment she reached her. 'Oh!!! My gosh you have gone old my lady.'

They laughed.

'Ohh, as if you are still the same old young and sexy darling,' Natasha said.

'Well, what can I do if the boys do not try on me any more (smiling),' Tia said, 'you know . . . monkeys never know the value of old and sexy bananas.'

Natasha laughed and said, 'You haven't changed a damn bit, still considering boys as the heel of your sandals.'

'Well you know, they never allowed me to stay alone. A new one always tried on me every-day.'

'Ya!! I remember that. Anyway sit.' Said Natasha, as she pointed out the bench.

They sat.

'And, what's going on in life?' Natasha asked. With a curiosity to know, what was her old buddy doing all this time.

'Well just nothing. I was growing my children twenty years ago and now am growing my grandchildren.' Tia replied. 'And, what about you? You seem to have changed a lot.'

Natasha gave a wistful look and said, 'Well!! Life is just going on. I have had all the happiness I ever needed and from the person who could have given me the best.'

Tia felt glum for her old, sublime friend. 'Ya. I heard about your husband's death,' Tia said. She locked her lips and the sadness for her friend flooded her heart, 'Sorry for that.'

'Ohh! No.' Natasha said, waving her hand to Tia. 'It's okay, don't be sorry . . . sorry is a word used for something bad or sad, but Ayush . . . he was only a joy, a beautiful part of my life. All of a sudden, he came from nowhere and changed my life in a moment. Being with him toughed me a new meaning of life, or else, I was just drowning with my past because of some useless people.'

Tia kept her hand on Natasha's shoulder, showing sympathy to her old friend whose eyes were wet with tears.

Natasha continued, 'There were no pain, no glumness and fear of anything till he was by my side.' Tears rolled out of her eyes one by one, her voice was much lower, softer and sadder. 'The only regret is that I will never be able to love him anymore, I will never have the hug that made me so secure and I'll never have anyone to understand me,' she paused and rubbed her tears, 'I'll never be able to have them again.'

Tia's heart was filled with more emotions. Tears started rolling down her eyes too. She was missing her husband, he was alive and with her, but, she knew that she did not have much time with him. All of a sudden, she wanted to live as many moments with him as she could; hug him, kiss him, cry with him, but more importantly love him.

They sat there for another hour recollecting memories of the last few years, comforting each other in sad memories and trying to re-live the days long gone.

People came in and left the garden, the leaves; yellow and green, felt on the ground as slowly as a walking tortoise, the early morning fog was still clearing the ground and sun was all set to shine brighter.

'Okay, guess I'll have to leave now,' Tia said. She kept her purse over her right shoulder.

'Sure,' Natasha said, 'it was nice seeing you after such a long time.' Tia held Natasha's hands.

'Same here,' Tia said.

Tia stood up to leave. Natasha turned her face to her grandson. Tia had just walked a few steps when she turned around and faced Natasha.

'Natasha,' she called her out loudly.

Natasha turned to face her. 'What happened?' Natasha asked

'Just wanted to say thank you,' Tia said.

'Thank you,' Natasha gave her a surprised look, 'for what?'

'For making me love my husband more than ever and for making me realise that how important are this last few moments of life that we have together.'

Tia gave her a friendly smile and started towards the gate. Natasha stood up from her place, looked around for a while and then headed to the grove of trees behind her.

The image of Ayush clicked in her mind when she first saw him at the coffee shop, images of the day when they would hardly talk, of their first night when things were just getting so worst and then of the moment they fell in love.

Tears rolled down her eyes as she entered the grove of trees, stepping on the fall leaves, she folded her hands and looked in-front, then to her left and right as if expecting to see her lost love (Ayush). As if he was right there, somewhere and would surprise her any moment. Her brain knew it wouldn't happen but her heart, it was expecting Ayush. It was glum and alone, it wanted to see that one face which would bring all the happiness and joy of the world in a matter of second.

She was feeling weak, not because of the stress but due to her memories. She touched a tree with her right hand and gaze at sky with locked lips, and then brought her looked down. She saw a yellow leaf which passed in-front of her eyes, fallen from the tree and making its journey to the ground. And her mind went back to old memories of her first night.

(IN NATASHA'S THOUGHT, 30 YEARS BACK)

Natasha stood up, walked to Ayush and sat next to him on the floor. They spoke nothing and kept their eyes fixed on the white wall behind the sofa, with only a small painting hung on it and two yellow night lamps on the sides.

Few minutes passed. Natasha turned to Ayush. She could see a strong feeling on his face, maybe it was sadness. He did not look anywhere else, except to the wall but she knew that it were only his eyes that were focusing on the wall but not his mind, it was lost somewhere else, it was not present in that room and with her. And at that moment, she looked into his eyes, deeper than she ever did. "Maybe he was right", she said to herself. She could see innocence in his eyes, as sense of truthfulness, but, along with it, she could see a lot more things. They were really like her; quiet, peaceful, but still sad, upset and lonely.

Ayush was lost in his world, trying to recollect his last moments with Anamika.

(IN AYUSH'S THOUGHT)

'That's it!!' Ayush was shocked. He loved Anamika like hell and now, she was breaking up their long relationship in a moment. 'Didn't this relation mean anything to you? Didn't you ever respect it?' he shouted but Anamika did not seem to care of him, she was busy closing the zip of her red bag. 'Am talking to you damn it,' Anamika picked up her purse from of dressing table, 'I said answer me!!' she kept her purse on top of her back and turned to Ayush.

'Listen, stop being so childish okay. And about our relation, well, it wasn't working anyway, so it's better we ended up right here,' Anamika said.

'It wasn't working? Well how can it work if you never tried to get it work?' Ayush said.

'Oh! So now you blame me for not making it work?' Anamika gave him a surprised look, 'listen it was you who always saw faults in me, and remember, that when a relationship one sees only fault it cannot work, so let me live and you live the life your way as simple as that.'

'What!!!! It looks simple to you?' Ayush was shocked, 'all the moments that we spend, love that I had for you, each and every moment cared I for you, do you think I will ever be able to forget it? And what faults are you talking of?' he went closer to Anamika, 'you never had time for our relationship. All you cared for was your work, and when I complained to you about that you do not give time to our relationship, it looks like a fault to you? It is a simple freaking truth.'

Anamika kept her hands over her head, took a deep breath, tried to calm down and said, 'Listen, Ayush, all this things you said, they show love and affection but they are a little bit crazy, and you should know how to respect time. When we are busy we work and when we are free we talk. I wanted to go out with you, two weeks back but you said you are busy, and I understood and didn't crib, did I? You must know how to respect time of other people.'

A tear dropped out of his eyes. His voice got softer and lower. 'True, Anamika. You are right. All this time I loved you like hell, I didn't even gave a damn to any of my stuff when you needed me. Do you think, I was always free when you needed me and I came running . . . no I wasn't free, I made my time for you damn it, I made myself available for you,' more tears left his eyes and his voice was much lower. 'I did all this for only one reason, and that is love. I love you more than anything in the world. And what are you doing? considering your own time and work over our love?' Anamika seemed tiered of this argument. She still considered his behaviour to be childish. She was not at all able to understand Ayush's love for her. All she wanted was to finish everything at that moment and get rid of the man who seemed to have been behind her so much.

'Listen,' she pointed a finger at Ayush. Her voice was gruff, 'I don't give a damn to anything at all. Just let me go and you live on and am sure that you will forget all this sooner or later and start minding your life like you used to mind it earlier.'

She picked up her bags. Ayush said nothing. He had no more words. He wanted to stop her but he knew it would not be possible. He could she her leaving his life forever with his wet eyes.

Anamika opened the door, got out side and closed it. Her hand was the last thing Ayush saw. He sat on the floor on his knees. He was shattered, not knowing what to do and not being able understand what just happened. He was not able to believe anything and he looked at the closed white door, as if, expecting Anamika to come back with smile on her pretty, innocent face saying that it was all a joke, but just after a moment, his heart told him that it was not to happen. She won't come back, it was all over.

'Fuckkk!!!' he shouted and took his head towards the floor. He cried louder and wished to cry louder, he wanted to get rid of this pain, and he wished that crying could have made something better of his situation but it wouldn't and he knew that.

Things seemed fine after he had talk with Anamika a few days back. She promised to never leave him and keep on loving him. Ayush did not want anything more from her or anybody else. Anamika loved him and that was enough for him. Anytime he had any doubting about her, he would just remember her words and calm down.

Things went on great for a few days, though Ayush doubted Anamika's love at times but he used to calm himself down. But, he could not do it for a long time. He could feel Anamika going away from him. His presence or absence hardly seemed to matter to her, and he would be dying to see her every day. He was not able to understand what was happening to his life, he was getting restless and furious.

Anamika would always give him an excuse; am not well so we will talk tomorrow, it is okay everything is fine between us, am busy, etc, when he tried to talk with her about their relationship. He was not happy by the fact that Anamika was ignoring their relations. She would talk to him a few times but of anything else other than their relation and for Ayush, sorting out the problem of their relationship was the only concern.

"LOVE DOES NOT HAPPEN WHEN YOU LIKE SOMEONE . . . BUT IT HAPPENS WHEN YOU FEEL SOMEONE."

—PRATIK HINDOCHA

CHAPTER 9

Ayush's gaze was still fixed on the wall but he was out of his thoughts, unaware of Natasha sitting next to him. For a moment he wondered where Natasha went, then, he turned to his right to see her sitting next to him.

He was surprised. Natasha's eyes were wet and her gaze was fixed on him. Maybe she was not aware that Ayush was looking at her or maybe she had a feeling, and that Ayush knew what she felt.

'Hey!! What happened,' Ayush asked with a friendly smile and soft voice.

Natasha got distracted by his voice. She felt ashamed for crying in-front of him. She turned her face and rubbed off her tears with her hand.

'Nothing, just missing family.' She said in a soft voice.

Ayush didn't think that was the case. In the last few hours, she had shown no sign of glumness or missing anyone and with the way she looked at him, he was sure that there was something else and he felt responsible to at-least know what was it and help her.

'Common, that cannot be the thing,' he gave her a friendly smile. 'You can trust me.' Natasha tried to relax and pretend as if nothing else was wrong.

'No, there is nothing else. It happens to every new bride,' Natasha said.

'Okay,' Ayush said.

What had happened to me, Natasha thought. She didn't know why she cried or what she saw in Ayush that made her cry. She felt that there were a lot of similarities in them but that does not mean that he might have been through the same things she went through. She was not even sure if she can trust Ayush or not, after all they have hardly met a few months back and talked even lesser. But then, her mind changed. She remembered that this man, who hardly know her, never behaved rude to her, nor did he complained about her rude behaviour and nor did he ever showed any anger on her. In fact he was always peaceful, quite and calm minded in everything. He was her husband. I must trust him as he has always been good to me and plus how can we live together if he does not know my biggest secret, she thought.

'Am sorry,' Natasha said. Ayush faced her.

'For what?' he asked.

'You are right,' they looked at each other, 'I am not missing my family. It's just something else.'

'I know that,' Ayush's cell-phone vibrated for the first time. He does not pick up. 'It's okay, it's your life. You can keep secrets if you want to.'

Second vibration.

'No. I actually wanna tell you.' Third vibration of the phone. 'There was a guy I fell in love with, a few years back.'

Fourth vibration of the phone.

'Okay, that's romantic. I didn't know you are a romantic?' he smiled. Fifth and last vibration.

Natasha smiled back and continued. 'His name was Sidharth. We met about two years back . . .'

(TWO YEARS BACK. SIDHARTH AND NATASHA AT THE RESORT)

Natasha had been standing at the resort reception for thirty minutes already. She was asked to wait there by the manager. She was angry and willing to take some action but she preferred waiting for Sidharth, who, had been missing for a while now. He called her more than two hours ago and said that, he was going to meet a friend and asked her to get ready as he was planning to take her for dinner, later along with his friend and friend's wife.

He called her after an hour and asked her to wait for him at the reception as he was already on his way. She did as told by him. She was in the reception room but Sidharth did not arrive, nor did he respond to her calls. She waited for a few minutes and thought it would be better for her to get back to her room. Sidharth would call her when he reaches, but the hotel staff did allow her to do so, without giving any specific reason.

She stood at the reception hall, looking here and there in her a black saree and the same colour blouse, which were perfect, match to her white skin and hair free underarms.

After about five more minutes, a female staff came to her and asked her to proceed to her room. Natasha returned her an angry look for making her wait for so long and then headed to her room.

She walked straight to her room, in angry mood through the lobby lighted with the yellow light. She passed to the first two brown room, and then through the next of set black doors and then the third. Then something happened. As she was about to open the door of her room straight in-front, someone kept a hand on her eyes.

Natasha was surprised, a sense of fear passed through her whole body. 'Who is it?' she said in a bit loud voice.

'Ssshh!!' she heard the voice. It was a male voice. 'It's your love,' the voice said.

Natasha felt a sense of relief in a second. She knew the voice, it was Sidharth's. 'What is this all about?' she asked in a soft tone.

'Just relax and see what I want to show you.' Sidharth said.

Sidharth took her a step ahead. Natasha heard the sound of the door; Sidharth opened the door. Natasha knew they were inside the room.

'Keep your eyes closed,' Sidharth said. And he took his hand off Natasha's eyes. She then took few steps forward.

'Remember, not to open your eyes,' Sidharth said.

Natasha heard the sound of Sidharth's lighter. 'Ohh! Common, what is it? Tell me?' Sidharth did not respond her. Natasha's eyes were closed for a while more, she was curious to know what Sidharth have for her.

'Open your eyes now,' Sidharth said.

She slowly opened her eyes to find herself in a dark room lightened with candles and flowers all around. A table was placed near their bed with food, two glasses, a bottle of champagne, a vase with roses and a candle in the middle.

'A perfect candle light, isn't it?' Sidharth asked. He stood behind Natasha with his back rested on the closed door, in full black outfits.

Natasha turned to him with a smile on her face and went close to him.

'And where is your friend and his wife.' She kept her hands on his chest.

Sidharth un-rested his back of the door and spoke in a soft voice. 'What friend? Don't tell me you really thought that I will ever let some friend disturb our privacy.' They smiled.

Sidharth pulled back the chair for Natasha (she sits) and then moved near his seat. He picked up the bottle of champagne and splashed opened it. He poured the yellow liquid into Natasha's glass and then filled his.

He took his seat and raised a toast to Natasha.

———

'. . . and that was our last time together.' Natasha ended.

It took more than thirty minutes for Natasha to speak out her full story. Not even for once in that time did Ayush took his eyes of her. His concentration was fixed on the innocent face in-front of him, her lost facial expressions which were trying to recollect each and every moment of that time, trying not to miss out any point and her red lips moving up and down as she uttered her words.

Ayush kept his hand on Natasha's shoulder. 'It's okay. These things happen.'

He stood up, walked slowly to the window and faced the full white moon. His heart was filled with sorrow and emotions, and he felt like crying out as loudly as could, at that very moment.

'What happened?' Ayush turned to face her. She saw sadness and a heart with secret in him with her clean eyes. 'You can share with me if you have something.' She paused and then continued in a soft, innocent and friendly voice. 'You can trust me.'

Ayush faced back at the moon and started. 'My story is just as same as yours . . . Her name was Anamika . . .'

(TWO YEARS BACK. AFTER ANAMIKA LEFT AYUSH)

Dusk was spreading its tentacles and the sun had almost set. The sky was yellow, red and orange. Ayush slowly walked on the wet sand of the beach on his bare feet and sandals in hand. He looked around, as if trying to search for peace of mind, but, he knew he won't find anything. Tears rolled down his eyes. He missed Anamika like hell. He was not ready to believe she had left him. He hoped that she would just come from no-where and hug him, but his mind knew it would not happen and his heart just drowned more into the deep thoughts of Anamika.

He wanted to shout, scream and kill himself hoping that, at-least something out of this would bring back his love.

He sat on the sand with his trousers folded and sandals next to him. His eyes were still wet and brain lost, then his eyes fell upon a young couple. The girl kept her head on boy's shoulder; they smiled and walked bare feet. He instantly imagined himself with Anamika.

He rolled up his feet, kept his hands on them and hid his head to avoid showing his tears to anyone.

[decorative symbol text]

"TODAY . . . LET SOMEONE LEAVE YOU, LET SOMEONE GIVE YOU TEARS, LET SOMEONE BREAK YOUR HEART AND LET SOMEONE GIVE TO THE WORST MEMORIES TO LIVE WITH . . . BUT REMEMBER THAT WHEN YOU MEET HER TOMMOROW, JUST DO NOT FORGET TO SMILE."

— *PRATIK HINDOCHA*

CHAPTER 10

He (Ayush) kept quiet and so did she (Natasha). He stood on the left end of the window, resting his left part of the body to the end with hands folded and Natasha was at the opposite end. Their eyes met, it didn't blink and nor did their gaze shift else-where. Their lips locked as they felt the soft air in their whole body. They had something to say, but there was no need to. Their gaze and the silence spoke everything.

A strong wind rushed in through the open glass window. Natasha's hair were in-front of her eyes. She took his eyes of Ayush due to this disturbance and turned her face to the left.

Ayush kept on looking at her. He enjoyed her gaze too. Suddenly a strong wind blew and Natasha turned her face. He walked to her. Her face was still on the left with hair covering the face and neck. He slowly got his hand up, took his fingers to her hair, cleared her face again and rested the hair behind her ears.

Without saying a word he went back. Natasha then brought back her focus on Ayush. Still no words just a silence and eyes meeting. Their gaze might have made the gods jealous; there came another strong wind which again covered her (Natasha's) eyes. Ayush again walked to her and again kept her hair behind her ears.

Natasha did not know what to say. She did not face him (shying) but she wanted to say something, but before she could speak herself out, Ayush spoke softly. 'I love you.'

She looked at him in surprise. Just for a moment she thought that Ayush had just spoken what was in her mind. He could hear her breath and she could hear his. Still no words and still the eyes locked with each other but the silence spoke a lot more then could have the voice.

Their lips moved closer, no push, they just did. They could now hear their breath more clearly; smell it and feel it. Just in a moment their lips were locked. He held her through her lower back and she kept her hands around his neck.

They separated their lips (but not too far). Their eyes met again, still no words but a tear of joy rolled through Natasha's eyes, passing through her white cheek and dropping on the ground. Then there was a smile on her face and on his as well. Their lips moved closer again and then locked, this time for much longer.

———

Ayush sat on the floor, his back supported by the bed. Natasha lied on top of him, resting her head on his waxed chest and playing with his night shirt buttons with her fingers.

'You know what . . .' she paused, '. . . I finely realise that I wasted all my time, the two freaking years, thinking of a person who was nothing more than a damn. He had no feelings for me, nothing at all,' Ayush held her hand and kissed it.' But, like a fool, I kept on thinking that he would be nice to me, he would come back to me and this mess will soon end . . . it didn't happen.' Her eyes were met.

'I know,' Ayush spoke,' I was a fool too. You know, wasting my time on some dump ass girl who hardly had any time for people who loved her. Her time was only for her work and money.'

Ayush took his cup of coffee and brought near his mouth to take a sip.

'Ooop!' he looks inside the white cup.

'What happened?' Natasha asked.

'It's already empty,' he said. 'Better ask for one more . . . what will you have?'

'A beer,' Natasha looked at him and smiled. Ayush gave her a surprised look.

'What!!'

———

Ayush dialled the room service number.

First ring. Anamika's image still touched his mind, but this time, he hardly seemed to care of it, he was finely able to force himself to throw it out.

Second ring.

Third ring.

It came as a surprise to him when Natasha asked for a beer, but he was glad to see the other part of her: free, chilled, worries free and impish.

Fourth ring,

Fifth ring,

'Hello. This is room service. How may I help you?' said a voice. This time it was a male voice.

'Well, yes,' Ayush spoke. 'This is room number one-zero-one . . . and I would like to have two cold beers please.'

The man noted down the order and said, 'okay, sir. Your order will reach you in ten minutes. Would you like to have anything to eat, sir.'

'Nop, this is fine. Just send it quick,' Ayush said.

'Sure sir.' Both kept back the phone.

(TEN MINUTES LATER)

The doorbell rang. Ayush asked Natasha to stand up from his lap, so that he can open the door. Natasha did the same.

Ayush stood up and headed for the door, looked through the key hole and opened it.

It was the same waiter. 'Come in my sir,' Ayush cracked a joke on waiter, knowing that he was surely fed up after serving them three times that night.

The waiter smiles at the joke cracked on him as he stepped in the room. He headed to the table in-front of the sofa and kept the trays containing the coffee on cups.

Natasha walked to Ayush as she saw the waiter heading to the table to keep the tray. She went to Ayush, stood next to him and kept her hands around him; through stomach. And he kept his left hand around her shoulder (holding the door with his right hand), and kissed her right cheek.

The waiter walked to them, left the room, stood outside the door, turned around and said, 'good night sir, ma'am.'

———

The waiter stood outside Ayush and Natasha's room. He was nervous about going inside the room of this couple and that too at this time of the night, and with the bottle of beers.

101. He read the number written in gold later and then rang the doorbell. He waited for a while. He then heard the sound of footsteps nearing the door, he knew it would open any second and it did.

The door opened and he saw the young groom in his night suit, standing in-front of him.

'Come in my sir,' Ayush said.

He (waiter) knew it was a joke but he didn't mind and instead returned him a smile. As he entered, his eyes felt back on the sublime Natasha. 'What a beauty,' he said to himself, as he saw Natasha heading to Ayush.

He kept the tray on the table, lifted the white cloth kept on the top of it, and while doing so, he turned his eyes to Natasha and Ayush, who looked in a romantic mood.

'Abe kitna romance karega. Thoda mereliye bhi to chodde (How much more will you romance her. Leave some for me as well),' he thought.

He was so freaking jealous of Ayush at that time. God, he wished to have Natasha so badly or he wished, even he had some beautiful bride as her. Ayush and Natasha took months to fall in love but this guy was already up for her when he saw her for the first time, it was **LOVE AT FIRST SIGHT** for him. Poor fellow, hope he knows that the most famous love stories of the world were never complete and his was now one of them.

He left the room and waited for the lift in-front of the steel doors with the image of his Aiswarya Rai still in mind.

——

'You know . . .' Natasha said. They sat on the edge of the window with the beer of bottle in their hand.' . . . I was totally in a horrible state after Sidharth had left me. I thought that it was the end of everything, all the happiness, love, a peaceful life and all the things which made my life beautiful.' Ayush kept on looking at her. Natasha looked outside at the white moon.' I didn't wanted anything,' she turned to face Ayush, 'not even marriage, but I eventually had to marry you for the sake of my family. I didn't want them to worry about me. Life was going like shit, and for a moment, I had thought, that, if my decision to marry was a big mistake?'

'And what do you think now?' Ayush asked softly. Natasha smiled.

'I think that, I won't regret my decision. I don't know what would have happened if I had not agreed to marry you.'

Ayush kept his bottle next to him on the edge of the window. 'Nothing wrong would have ever happened. You know, things in life happen for good, so, if we really were to meet, we would have eventually met in anyway, may be today or tomorrow, as a husband and wife, friends or strangers.'

'True,' Natasha agreed. Ayush took a sip of his bottle.

'You know. My life did not seem to go anywhere as well. I even thought of suicide, but as it is said "Better said than done", it was a crap idea . . .'

'And cowardly too,' Natasha interrupted. Ayush smiled.

'. . . Agreed. Totally a coward act.' They took a sip of their beers. 'So, tell me. How did your ex-boyfriend look like? I mean was he hotter than me?' they laughed.

'Ah, no,' Natasha said', and you know, it's not about looking good but more about having a good heart to love, which, I am sure he did not have.'

They did not speak for a while and kept their eyes fixed at the beautiful moon.

'What do you have to say about a dance?' Ayush asked after momenst of silence.

'What?' Natasha said. Surprised.

'Dance. You know, it's a beautiful, silent night with a lovely moon.'

'Okay, but, where is the music?' Natasha said.

Sidharth walked to the sofa where he had kept his laptop. He switched it on.

"NEVER TAKE ANYBODY'S LOVE AND AFFECTION FOR YOU FOR GRANTED BECAUSE ONE DAY YOU WILL DIE FOR IT AND ONE DAY YOU WILL REALISE THAT WHY DID THEY LOVED YOU SO MUCH."

—*PRATIK HINDOCHA*

CHAPTER 11

Sidharth raised his left hand, straight towards Natasha. Natasha gave him a smile and kept her bottle on the edge of the window next to Ayush's bottle.

Natasha walked to him and stood at a small distance. She then placed the palm of her left hand on the top of his left raised hand and went closer to him as the soft music played on the laptop. They were close to each other; their bodies touching. Ayush brought his right hand around Natasha's lower back, and she kept her hand on Ayush's back. It was so different, Ayush wearing night shirt and pant, and Natasha wearing her sleeveless night gown.

They danced . . . without looking anywhere else, except into each other's face and a light smile never left their face. They knew they finely had what they always wanted to have; someone who would love them back equally. They were sure that a trust was built which will never break; no wonder what ever obstacles came into their way. This trust was not because they were already married and secured, as, a divorce was always an option, but because of something, something inside their heart which said that "This is it. Their entire wait for happiness, trust and love was finely over; that they could rely on each other, that they could be sure that from that moment they will have someone by their side who would always be there in the time of trouble and to wipe out any tear which came in their eyes". They were sure, at peace and relaxed for everything.

'Do you miss her now?' Natasha asked. They looked into each other's eyes.

'No . . .' Ayush paused and then continued,' . . . for the first time, I did not even think of her. I never will.' They smiled. 'Do you miss him?' Ayush asked.

'No,' Natasha answered, 'just same as you. For first time I didn't, I never will.'

They did not speak a word after that. Just looked into each other's eyes and felt the happiness inside. They were still not ready to believe that last five to six hours had changed their life completely. Every pain and sorrow they were going through was gone. The life had totally changed; they did not even remember how it felt to be in a gloomy state of mind.

They moved their lips closer and closer, and in no time, they locked together as never to separate them. Natasha's hands were around Ayush's neck, and Ayush kept his hand around her back. They kissed passionately, as if, they had waited of this for years, and they surely did.

Ayush un-locked their lips, and took his face bit aback.

'What happened?' Natasha asked him.

Ayush smiled and spoke. 'We need to do something.'

'What?' Natasha asked him surprisingly.

'Wait here,' Ayush said.

———

Ayush lifted the small white table near the bed and kept it in-front Natasha, right in the middle of the room, and walked to the dressing table and picked a candle (not burning any more) kept on it, and kept it on the top of the table (kept in-front of Natasha). He brings out a lighter from his pocket and lights the candle

'What are you doing?' Natasha asked him curiously.

Ayush walked to Natasha and held her hand.

'What do think about a private marriage?' Natasha laughed.

'What are saying,' she said, still laughing,' we have already married.'

Ayush held another of her hands with his hand and spoke. 'True . . . we have already married, but did it look like one?'

Natasha's laughter disappeared but not the smile of her face. She got what Ayush was trying to say. They married and made the promises but while they were doing it, they were not in love and nor were they serious about keeping those promises. So, now, since they have finely started liking each-other, it was not a bad idea to have a personal and different marriage and make the promises they will never break.

A tear rolled through out of Natasha's right eye. 'Let us do it,' she said.

Ayush held her right hand with his left and Natasha stood behind him. Ayush took a step backward and stood next to her.

'What are doing,' she asked politely.

'I love you, and I will always want you to walk with me in every aspect of life and not behind me.' They smiled to each other.

They started for the first PHERA or round (a part of ritual in Indian wedding), holding each other's hand and looking into the eyes, with a happy smile on the face. They completed the first round when Ayush suddenly stopped. He turned to Natasha and said.

'Every phera means a promise to your partner. I do not know what those promises are but I would make our promise and will keep them for ever . . .' he paused and then continued' . . . my first promise to you is that **I WILL NEVER LEAVE YOU ALONE IN ANY PHASE OF LIFE.'**

Natasha's eyes were filled with tears again. Ayush rubbed her tears with his hand and started to walk but Natasha held his hand tightly and did not move.

'What happened?' Ayush asked.

'You forgot about my promise,' she said, '**GOOD OR BAD, WE WILL FACE EACH AND EVERY SITUATION TOGETHER.'** Ayush smiled.

They walked for their second phera, in the same way as they walked earlier one. They stopped after completing it and Ayush made his second promise.

'**THERE WILL ONLY BE ONE PERSON I WILL EVER BE WITH AND THAT IS YOU,'** he promised.

'**MY LOVE FOR YOU SHALL NEVER DECREASE,'** Natasha promised. They walked for their third phera.

They could feel the hand of one another and the happiness in the eyes. They slowly moved step by step, without any hurry, knowing what that moment meant and that there will never ever be any sublime moment than that.

The third phera came to an end. They faced each other.

'THE ONLY TEARS YOU WILL DROP FROM NOW ON-WARDS WILL BE OF JOY AND HAPPINESS,' Ayush promised.

'THE ONLY MOMENT WHEN YOU WILL LEAVE MY HEART WOULD THE ONE WHEN IT WILL NO LONGER BE PUMPING.' Natasha promise. They walked for the fourth phera.

The fresh air that touched their body seemed fresher than ever before. There was nothing in the world which could have side-tracked their joy, nothing at all.

The fourth phera came to its end. They faced one another and Ayush made his promise.

'YOUR SMILE SHALL ALWAYS BE MY FIRST PRIORITY.'

'I SHALL CONSIDER YOUR HEART AS MINE AND DO NOTHING THAT WILL HURT IT,' Natasha promised.

They moved for the fifth phera with their eyes in tears, the tears of joy and they held their hands tighter to make sure that nothing separated them, a sign of an un-spoken promise.

'I WILL STAY AWAKE AND SIT NEXT TO YOU WHEN YOU ARE SICK, HUG AND KISS YOU WHEN YOU ARE LOW AND I WILL TAKE YOU FAR AWAY WHERE THERE WILL BE ONLY ME AND YOU,' Ayush promised, after the end of the fifth phera.

'I PROMISE YOU THAT, YOU WILL ALWAYS HAVE A FEELING INSIDE YOU WHICH WILL

SAY THAT NO ONE COULD HAVE EVER LOVED YOU MORE THAN ME,' Natasha promised. And they walked for the sixth phera.

It was the most beautiful part of their life to hear such nice and trustful words from their partner. Though they heard many such fake words and promises, but this time, something inside them told that this was not a fake. It was for real and to last forever and ever. They came to the end of sixth one.

'I SHALL NEVER DOUBT ON YOU FOR ANYTHING AND YOU SHALL HAVE ALL THE FREEDOMS THROUGHT YOUR LIFE.' Ayush promised.

'FROM NOW ON, YOU SHALL BE THE OTHER GOD I WILL EVER KNOW EXCEPT FOR THE ONE SITTING ON THE SKY,' Natasha promised.

They walked for the seventh and final phera and to make the final promise.

The seventh phera ended. They looked into one another's eyes which were still in the tears of joy for what had happened in last few moments. Ayush did not know what to say. He knew that there was no number of promises which was enough for her; such was the depth of their love. He thought for a while, thought what to tell her that will be more than any other promise in the whole world, and them a line came in his mind. He knew that there could never be any word better than those.

He sat on one knee, like the heroes do in the film, and raised his hand to Natasha.

'I LOVE YOU,' he said, with a soft and innocent tone.

More tears rolled out of Natasha's eyes. She kept her hand on his and slowly sat on her knees too. They moved closer till their foreheads met with tears shining on their cheeks. Natasha was not able to speak. She was still trying to believe it was all true; the moment, the man, their promise, and her new and happy life.

She spoke slowly and softly. **'I LOVE YOU TOO.'**

They hugged, with tears and smile, like mad, who looked for a hug since the centuries. They moved their hands behind each-other's back and cried loudly and the only word they spoke was **I LOVE YOU/I LOVE SO MUCH.**

———

The sun shone high on the sky and fell directly on the two (still in each—other's arm on the floor) through the open window.

They slowly separated with their eyes meeting and the tears shining on their cheek due to the sun light. They stood while holding their hand and speaking nothing, there were no words to speak. Everything was being said with tears of joy leaving the eyes and a beautiful silence. Just no words, no words needed at all, for that wonderful moment and true love; there was no need of anything. Their hearts knew what was being said and what was being heard. Just a silence was required to make all lovelier than it was, just a silence.

(TWO HOURS LATER)

They walked through the white hotel lobby, shining due to the sun light coming in from the window. Natasha rested her head on Ayush's left shoulder, and Ayush's hand coming around from her back. They were leaving for their home. Ayush carried a black bag on his right hand.

Almost twelve hours ago, they walked through the same place towards the same room like two un-known that saw each other a hundred times in last few months but were more than strangers. And now, they walk knowing about each-other more than anybody else did and with a total faith upon one-another, and of course, with heart and mind which were loving, burden free, joyful and at peace.

'You know what?' Natasha spoke, 'I was thinking. What would I say if any of my friends asked me that, whether we slept on our first night or had fun.' She paused and then continued. 'Guess what I'll have to say is that, we did not sleep but also did nothing at all.' Ayush smiled.

'Or, maybe there is a better answer . . . that we fell in love with another,' Ayush said, and they walked on a long journey **together**.

THE POEM BELOW IS IN HINDI. I KNOW
THAT IT WILL NOT BE UNDERSTOOD BY
ALL BUT I DON'T THINK THAT I SHOULD
TRANSLATE IT AS I DO NOT HAVE PROPER
WORDS WITH FEELING TO DO IN ANY
OTHER LANGUAGE.

SARI RAAT USE DEKHTA RAHA,
USKI KHUBSURATI KO MAIN DOORSE HI
SARHATA RAHA.

USKE GALO KO APNE HOTHO SE MILANE
KI THI
DIL ME JO KHWAHIS,
RAAT BHAR USE MAIN DABATA RAHA.

USKE SUKUN BHARE CHEHRE SE MAIN
BHI KHUSH
HOTA RAHA,
AUR USKI BANDH ANKHO SE MEIN NAZRE
MILATA RAHA.

WOH DEKH RAHITHI SAPNE APNI BANDH
ANKHO SE,
MAIN TO USE HI APNA SAPNA BANATA
RAHA.

JANTE HUVE BHI KI USKI KHUSI KISI AUR
SE HAI,
YEH DIL KAMBAKHAT USE HI APNI KHUSI
BANATA RAHA.

'CHERISH EACH AND EVERY MOMENT WITH THE PEOPLE YOU LOVE AND THE PEOPLE WHO LOVE YOU, BECAUSE ONE DAY . . . YOU WILL ONLY HAVE THEIR MEMORIES TO LIVE WITH.'

—*PRATIK HINDOCHA*

CHAPTER 12

The old and lonely Natasha stood between the big trees in the garden below the cloudy sky. She looked up at the sky and closed eyes to see Ayush's face inside her heart.

A drop of water felt on her right cheek, she opened her eyes and touched the drop with her hand and looked at it. There came a second drop, then third, fourth, fifth and then thousands all-together with quick speed, wetting her full body. She looked in-front and saw Ayush coming out of the trees with smile on face his, raising his hand to her, as if asking her to take the joy of the beautiful shower. He walked to her, step by step, and she (Natasha) smiled but with lots of tears. She ran to him and hugged him tightly.

'I love you . . . I really love,' she told him,' I miss you alot, please don't leave me, this life is nothing without you.'

Ayush kissed on her forehead and spoke, 'I love you too.' He released her, took her a step away, looked inside her and continued,' you know something, am never away, I' am always with you all the time, in each and every breath of yours.' He rubbed Natasha's tears. 'I see you all time. But you know what; I can never live,

I can't, because my life is in your smile.' Natasha spoke nothing, she just wanted to hear him, his voice and admire him, 'and if you don't smile then how do you expect me to live every day. Remember that day when you told me that my heart is yours?'

'Yes I do,' Natasha spoke in a sad tone.

'And what are you doing now? You cry so much and give pain to my heart. It (heart) cannot see you suffer, it only wants to see you happy and joyful.'

'Am sorry for that,' Natasha said.

'Don't be. Just remember, that if want to keep alive inside you then you must never drop tears of your eyes. Just live happily, cheerfully, being impish all day and feel me inside your heart,' their eyes were wet, 'and I shall always live . . . live inside you and for you.'

He spoke this and they hugged tightly, with tears. Natasha did not want to leave him, she just wanted to stick with him, but then, she could not feel his body anymore, and she could not feel any hands around her and her hold got softer. She slowly opened her eyes and looked around in search of her love but found only trees and rain water.

It was her fantasy. Natasha smiled and her eyes were wet. She was glum and lonely, but she had no complains, because in the end, she was grateful to god for giving her the most wonderful person ever, who kept her happy till he lived and never let a tear come in her eyes.

She faced up at the sky, with closed eyes and speared her hands. Drops of water fell on her face and the palm of her hand one after another as a light smile and tears appeared on her face.

'I miss you so much,' she spoke in a glum voice. She was crying. She wished she had him at that moment, so that she could have hugged him and cried her heart out. She wanted to have him in her arms and rest her head on his laps, and close her eyes peacefully but she knew it will never happen.

'I promise, I will always smile and live the way you want me to live **and I will always keep you alive inside me, in a corner of my heart . . . I PROMISE.'**

———

(FIFTEEN YEARS LATER)

Natasha; white hair, swollen cheeks and wrinkles with dark circle, in her white night gown. Sat on her wheel chair in-front of the window, facing the open door of her room. She was older, there were only a few things in her room; a brown bed white mattress, pillow and black blanket—a cupboard with brown door—a dressing table with a big mirror and a wooden chair in-front—and a few books on her bed.

She could she someone heading towards her, but her eyes were too old to the see was it. She tried to see the person better but couldn't and she did not even have her glasses in her hand. The image was shabby but it was getting clear and clear as the person neared. Finely she could she who it was when the person stood in-front of her chair.

It was her grandson, Rahul. He was in London since last five years, and Natasha was more of lonely to not have him next to her. Her boy had really grown. He was about six feet, with black spiked hairs, wearing black suit, shirt and pant, and his smiling face brought a lot of peace to her eyes.

He touched Natasha's feet and sat on one knee in-front of her. 'How is my beauty doing?' he asked her.

'Oh! Just getting sexier with age,' Natasha joked. They gave laughter.

Ayush stood up, sat on the bed and turned Natasha's wheelchair to him. They talked and talked for an hour. Natasha was feeling better after a long time.

'Grand ma,' Rahul said, 'remember you were telling me a romantic story years ago in the garden and I left it because I found it boring.'

'Oh yes. I remember that one my child. Why do you ask of it?' Natasha said.

'Well . . .' he paused, 'can you please complete it today,'

A light smiled appeared on Natasha's face. She could not have said no, even if she had to speak of it a million times. 'Of course my son. As many time as you want to listen it.'

Rahul turned her chair towards the window and she loved outside at the greenery and the rain water falling from the sky.

'Well,' she spoke, 'long time ago . . .'

What was it? Their destiny or luck. May be nothing of that short. It was just a magic, a magic which brought two un-known and hopeless people together from different walks of their life and changed it (life) completely in the matter of hours.

It is truly said, that you don't expect the timing of love. It just happens anywhere; anyhow, with anyone and un-expectedly with someone you never thought of, and just within a fraction of seconds, it changes your life completely. You would suddenly start having a wonderful feeling, your pains and sufferings of past are gone and all you want is that one person who's presence makes your life so wonderful.

. . . and they lived happily ever after.' Those were the last word that came out of Natasha's mouth, and then she lay lifeless on her wheelchair, with her head bent to her left, eyes open and a smile on her face.

Her dead eyes could she Ayush standing outside the window in the rain, raising his hand to her with a smile on his face. Natasha was young again, the same twenty seven year old. She ran to him and gave him her hand. They smiled at each other, looked into eyes and they walked in the rainbow towards the heaven to life forever and together.

'Will we always be together now?' Natasha asked him.

'Yes, forever,' Ayush smiled to her and they held their hands tightly.

Natasha kept her head on his shoulder and Ayush kept his hand around her back, and they walked on the colourful lights of the rainbow, never to separate.

"LOVE IS TRULY A MAGIC, A MAGIC WHICH HEALS ALL YOUR PAIN WITH ONE HUG, MAKES YOU FEEL SECURED WHEN YOU ARE BETWEEN TWO ARMS, MAKES YOU HAPPY WHEN YOUR TEARS ARE RUBBED BY SOFT HANDS, GIVES YOU AN AMAZING FEELING WHEN YOU WALK HAND IN HAND WITH HEAD RESTED ON A TRUSTED SHOULDER, DESTROYS ALL THE FEAR WHEN A BEAUTIFUL FACE COMES IN-FRONT OF YOU AND MOST IMPORTANTLY, IT REPAIRS EVERY WOUND WHEN IT (LOVE) COME IN YOUR LIFE."

—*PRATIK HINDOCHA*